UNREASONABLE DOUBT

UNREASONABLE DOUBT

Elizabeth Ferrars

CHIVERS LARGE PRINT
BATH

British Library Cataloguing in Publication Data available

This Large Print edition published by Chivers Press, Bath, 2001.

Published by arrangement with Peter MacTaggart.

U.K. Hardcover ISBN 0 7540 4616 8
U.K. Softcover ISBN 0 7540 4617 6

Copyright © Elizabeth Ferrars, 1958

Printed and bound in Great Britain by
BOOKCRAFT, Midsomer Norton, Somerset

UNREASONABLE DOUBT

CHAPTER ONE

The July evening was a fine one. Another fine one. Such weather, thought Professor Dirke, as he started the short walk from his home to the Maybush, could not possibly last much longer.

But as it happened, it did not matter to him personally whether it lasted or not. In three days' time he would be in the South of France. And for others, no doubt, it would be best if the drought were not to continue. Looking at his neighbours' gardens, he noticed that in the last day or two the grass had acquired an unfamiliar brownish tinge, that the dark earth looked grey and dusty, and that flowers that should have been in their prime were shrivelling before they had opened.

That morning he had seen a notice in the post office, prohibiting the use of water in the gardens.

'Rain, rain—we need rain,' he said.

He spoke half-aloud, but entirely insincerely. For the sake of his own garden he would have been delighted if a few heavy showers could have fallen in the dead of night. Yet how could anyone, whose senses responded to sunshine and warmth and to a sky of tranquil brightness, honestly want such weather to end? How could anyone, during weeks which had been almost as golden and calm as the fabulous summers of everyone's childhood, start crying for rain?

But Alistair Dirke did not pretend to be any sort of a countryman. He had been born in a London suburb. He had been educated at University College School and at London University. He had been lecturer, senior lecturer and reader in universities in various northern industrial cities. Then, thankfully, he had returned, as professor of social anthropology, to a London college, and, given a free choice, he would probably still have been living in London.

Not that he was dissatisfied with life in the village of Rollway. He was one of the fortunate people who can work in trains, so the journey was no disadvantage to speak of; the small Georgian house, with its quiet garden and its view of the downs, was a delight; the neighbours were pleasant; the Maybush was pleasant. And Rose, so she said, was happy. Happy and grateful because he had given her so much of what she wanted.

To have been anything but satisfied would have been highly unreasonable, and Alistair, for a professor, was a rather reasonable man. That is, until the last few weeks, he had assumed that that was what he was, though at the moment his security in the belief was a little shaken. As the long shining days of this most remarkable summer in living memory had followed one another, his own private horizon had been darkened by a growing cloud, and a cloud so unlikely to have any real existence in his clear sky, and so preposterous in shape, that he could explain it only as the product of a hysterical imagination.

Fortunately, the cloud was not yet a very large one. By a slight exercise of will, he was able at most times to ignore the shadow it cast. Earlier that evening it had been much on his mind, interfering with his attempt to work on some statistics that he had collected on the way that the agricultural labourer spends his wages, but now, walking towards the Maybush, and pausing to look at the herbaceous border in the vicarage garden, his mind was almost as serene as he felt that it should be. Or so he managed to convince himself, as he dropped the stub of his cigarette on the ground and conscientiously set his foot upon it, since in weather like this it would be the easiest thing in the world to start a fire. Yet the truth about him was that as he did so, he looked rather as if he were planting a foot on a fallen enemy; an enemy, furthermore, who might yet rise up and smite

3

him.

If he had no awareness of this, it was in the main because he had very little awareness of his appearance, though, on the whole it was attractive and distinctive. At forty-four he was a slight, quick-moving man of medium height, with a crest of thick brown hair above a high narrow forehead, grey eyes of singular brightness and intentness, thin cheeks, a long chin and a friendly and responsive manner.

Reaching the Maybush, he found the door standing wide to let in as much coolness as possible. In the bar was the usual crowd of known and half-known faces, and among them, as he had expected, that of Henry Wallbank, whose eyes met his as he entered.

They said good evening to each other, then in apparent surprise, Henry said, 'Rose not with you?'

He was a tall, bald man of about fifty-five, with a heavily lined face, covered with minute red veins, heavy pouches under his eyes and rimless spectacles that never sat quite straight on his short broad nose. With his chin nestling between the wings of a high stiff collar, his loose-fitting suit of shepherd's plaid, and his stringy black tie, he always made Alistair feel that he must have stepped out of the illustration of some old and faintly musty book. In fact, it was from a museum

4

that he had emerged. He was Director of the Purslem Collection, a collection of furniture, pictures, porcelain and other precious things, housed in one of the big houses of the neighbourhood.

'She's gone to a W.I. meeting,' Alistair answered him. 'How's Agnes?'

Automatically, if one met Henry, one asked how Agnes Wallbank was.

'Not too good, not really good at all. Her back again,' Henry answered. 'I'll have to tell them in the meeting to-night that I don't think she'll be able to help at all at the fête. Alistair . . .' He moved his face closer to Alistair's ear. 'I'd like a word with you afterwards. Something's come up I'd like to discuss with you. Perhaps we could walk home together after the meeting.'

'Of course, but Rose may be picking me up here, if the W.I. meeting's finished in time,' Alistair said.

'Nothing she shouldn't hear,' Henry said. 'Hoped to see her, anyhow. Best like that, really. . . .'

He broke off as some other members of the committee of the Rollway Village Produce Association, which was to meet that evening in the Maybush, to discuss some final arrangements for the annual fête and flower show in the village, came in at the door.

The meeting, as usual, was held in a back room of the Maybush. The business dealt with seemed to Alistair immensely complicated, but so it did at all meetings of the Association. Listening to the secretary recalling arrangements agreed upon the month before for the hiring of marquees, the printing of posters to advertise the fête, the purchase of ice-cream and minerals, the movement of tables from the village hall to the field where the fête was to be held, and for returning them safely from the field to the village hall, the nominating of people to take charge of the various side-shows, and so on, it occurred to him that most of the complexity arose from the fact that there was a traditional way in which all these activities had to be performed, and tradition, while simplifying everything wonderfully if you understood it, was the very devil if you didn't.

The meeting turned out a long one, as such meetings always did, and it was dusk already when he and Henry started walking homeward together, a hot still dusk, with a greenish glow in the sky and no leaf stirring.

A group of young men and girls from South Rollway, the Council estate that had recently been added to the village, and was the source of most of its more spectacular problems, were chattering noisily on a corner, but once Alistair and Henry had passed these, the road ahead of them was quiet and empty.

'Can't last much longer, this weather,' Henry observed as they walked along. 'Oughtn't to want it to, really. Poor look-out for the flower show if we don't get some rain soon. And they say the water situation in Manchester is getting serious.'

'All situations in Manchester are serious,' Alistair said.

'Eh?' Henry said uncertainly, and they walked on a little way in silence. Then Henry remarked, 'Rose didn't come.'

'No,' Alistair said.

'Probably had all she could take and gone straight home. Crime, really, to spend an evening like this indoors.'

'This thing you wanted to talk about . . .'

'Oh, yes. It's a favour I wanted to ask,' Henry said. 'If it's true you're going to Monte Carlo for your holiday.'

'Well, we're going to Cap Martin.'

'Lucky fellow. Can't remember when I got abroad last. Don't even bother to get my passport renewed now. No good trying it with Agnes the way she is. No good suggesting it, even. She always agrees, of course, then gets so excited at the idea it crocks her up.' Henry's voice was heavy and gloomy.

7

'Anything's better than that, especially after that last operation. Made things worse rather than better, I believe.'

To comfort him, Alistair said, 'It's just a habit with us, going abroad. And, of course, it gives Rose a break in the housekeeping. But with weather like this, I'd really just as soon stay at home.'

'Can't last much longer, can't possibly,' Henry said. 'This favour now, it's mainly because of Agnes I'm asking it. If I could go myself. . . . Well, I could, I suppose. Could fix up with someone to stay with her, though she'd say she'd be all right alone. But I'd worry about her all the time. You know how it'd be.'

'I'll be glad to do anything I can,' Alistair said.

'No, wait till you've heard what it is,' Henry said. 'Matter of fact, it's rather a lot to ask. I'm aware of that. So I'd sooner you and Rose talked it over a bit before you say yes, because I don't want to mess up your holiday for you. Don't want you to take it on at all unless it's got a sort of interest for you.'

Alistair's heart sank. He wanted his holiday to be a holiday, a matter of swimming and lying in the sun, of eating, drinking and reading detective stories. He did not want to do anything for anybody, least of all anything

8

interesting. Interesting things demanded thought.

'I'll do anything I can,' he said.

Henry shook his head. 'Talk it over between you first. It's about—'

'Wait a minute,' Alistair said. 'Why not come in and tell Rose about it yourself, then we'll give you an answer straight away.'

'But isn't it rather late? Perhaps she'll have gone to bed already.'

'Not for hours yet. Come in and have a drink.'

'Very good of you,' Henry said. 'If you're sure . . . Don't want to be a trouble to you, but if I could talk it over with you both. . . .'

They had just reached the turning where the road led to Henry's home. He wavered slightly towards it, but then, with an absent air, walked on beside Alistair.

It was to this point, later, that Alistair's thought returned when he asked himself how he might conceivably have avoided involving himself in the events that resulted from the request that Henry Wallbank was presently to make to him and Rose. Yet this was only because of the all too obvious symbolism of the two roads. In fact, by the time that they had reached the branching of the ways, it was already too late for Alistair to save himself from what was to follow.

9

For how can you refuse a favour to a man like Henry Wallbank, a sad, vague, ineffectual man with a wife like Agnes, a man whose mere presence near you makes you feel strong, competent and almost culpably fortunate?

From the moment when the favour had been asked, from the moment, even, when the thought of it had been born in Henry's mind, your consent could be taken for granted, your power to refuse it wholly discounted. Particularly if you are not, at the best of times, very good at saying no.

This fact that he was not good at saying no, that he suffered under what Rose had often described as an infuriating compulsion to oblige other people, Alistair blamed on the slowness of his mind. Some time after a request had been made and acceded to by him, he would find himself inventing ingenious excuses, which would have protected him from having to do what he did not want to do, without hurting anybody else's feelings. But these useful ideas never presented themselves at the moment of crisis. Far from it, at the time he often seemed actually to hurl himself at his fate, as, for instance, this evening, when he had actually pressed Henry to come home with him for a drink. For what could there have been against accepting the suggestion that Rose and he should discuss the matter in private before giving any answer?

But when eventually Alistair asked himself these questions, the disturbing thought came to him that a reason, indeed, a strong reason, had existed, causing him to press Henry to go home with him. The reason had been that Alistair had felt half-sure of what he would find when he reached home, and had had some muddled idea that to have someone with him when he found it would somehow deaden its effect upon him. That had been the cause of it all. That was why, in a way, he was to blame for all that followed. He had taken Henry home with him to protect himself.

However, as Alistair might have expected if he had thought more clearly and more honestly of what he was doing, Henry's presence had no protective effect at all. When Alistair saw what he had feared, when he saw the chairs in the dense shadow under the cherry tree in the garden, with the dim figure of Rose in one chair and that of Paul Eckleston in another, nothing could have protected Alistair from the stupefying attack made on his mind by his own feelings. Nothing could have prevented the small threatening cloud on his private horizon from spreading stormily over his whole sky.

CHAPTER TWO

None of this appeared on Alistair's face as he started to stroll across the lawn. Yet he had paused for just a moment, feeling impelled to drive both his hands deep into his pockets, keeping them imprisoned where they could make no further betraying gestures. Concerned with producing his normal smile and his normal tone of voice in greeting Paul Eckleston, Alistair himself was hardly aware that this had happened.

Paul had got to his feet. He was a trim, tall man of about Alistair's age, though he looked older, partly because his hair, grey already, what was left of it, had receded far back from his high, rounded forehead, and partly because of the fine lines fanning out from the corners of the grey eyes behind the horn-rimmed spectacles. These lines were of the kind that come early to any mobile and nervous face, but at first glance they added years to his appearance. He had strongly marked dark eyebrows and a wide, sensitive mouth. He was wearing flannel trousers, a checked shirt with the sleeves rolled up and no jacket.

Rose, still in her chair, smiled up at Henry Wallbank, said good evening and asked how

Agnes was.

When she had been told about Agnes's back, she said to Alistair, 'We need more chairs—and drinks, of course. I was just going to do something about them for Paul and me, but now I can leave them to you.'

Her smile strayed from Henry's face to her husband's. She had a serene air, looking relaxed and indolent in the garden chair, one bare arm bent behind her head. But you could never quite tell with Rose. That look of calm could sometimes mask an extraordinary degree of tension, and of late it had often seemed to do so. She was a tall woman, thirty-eight years old, fairly slender about the hips, so that she looked well in straight, simple clothes, such as the dark blue cotton dress that she was wearing now, though she was built in general with a certain solidity. Such grace as she had came from unhurrying, unselfconscious movements, much as the beauty that Alistair saw in her face, with its full, warmly coloured cheeks, its rounded chin and brown intelligent eyes, came from the way that it expressed the qualities in her that he loved.

He went for the chairs and the drinks and Paul went with him to help, while Henry, with a little sigh, subsided into the chair that Paul had left. When Paul and Alistair

13

returned, Paul carrying the chairs and Alistair the whisky and glasses, Rose and Henry were talking in voices that sounded dreamy and disembodied in the deepening shadow under the tree.

'Envy you,' Henry was saying. 'Years since I've done anything of the sort myself. Not since before the war. Used to go to Italy then, quite often. Not so expensive in those days, of course. Ah well.'

'It's a lot of bother, though,' Rose replied, playing down for Henry's sake, as Alistair had a little earlier, her pleasure in the thought of their holiday. 'I don't know why we don't just stay at home. What could be nicer than this? But it's impossible to make Alistair take any sort of a rest unless we go away. He finds reasons to go up to London every few days, or starts writing a book or something.'

Henry turned to Paul. 'And you're going abroad too, I expect,' he said enviously.

Alistair, setting the tray down on the grass and stooping over it to pour out the drinks, asked, 'Or are you staying put, like a sensible man?'

He was wondering when Paul had arrived here. Had he met Rose in the village, on her way back from the Women's Institute meeting, or had he called here, guessing that he would find her alone? Not that it mattered.

14

How could it matter?

'I take my holidays in the winter,' Paul answered, 'and keep them strictly urban.'

He had a soft, deep, carefully controlled voice, without much expression.

'London, Paris, Rome,' Henry murmured, as if he were mentioning fabulous cities, to be reached only by those who were possessed of magic carpets, while Alistair, with a flicker of contempt in his mind, wondered how Paul distinguished his work from his holidays.

That this thought might be highly unfair to Paul Eckleston, who made, and somehow sold, a quantity of what Alistair, in his ignorance, called pottery, over which, for all that Alistair knew, Paul sweated blood, even if he did not live on what he earned by it, was a fact of which Alistair was perfectly aware. But it did not lessen the satisfaction that his scorn momentarily gave him.

He supposed that because of Paul's presence, Henry would not tell them what it was that he wanted Rose and himself to do in Monte Carlo. Either he would leave it until next day, or try to out-stay Paul, for the favour that he wanted to ask had sounded at least moderately confidential. It seemed faintly surprising, therefore, when after a few minutes of disjointed discussion of the continuing drought, Henry said, 'Must tell you,

15

Rose, why I dropped in like this. Something's come up, something you might be able to do for me in Monte Carlo. I started to tell Alistair about it. Thought he could then discuss it with you and see how you both felt about it, but he suggested coming along and telling you about it myself. Very good of him. I'd be glad to know straight away, of course, how you both feel, just so long as you say frankly if it's too much trouble. Then I'll think of some other way of handling it.'

Rose arched her eyebrows faintly at Alistair, to which he replied with as blankly noncommittal a look as he could manage.

Henry looked thoughtfully from one to the other, then said, 'Suppose you haven't, either of you, ever heard of a man called Nikolo Pantelaras?'

Rose shook her head. Alistair felt that there was a certain familiarity about the name, but at first could not account for it. Then, as Henry went on, he began to recollect some gossip that he had heard in the village.

Henry had turned to Paul. 'You have, haven't you?'

'Naturally,' Paul answered. 'I remember him quite well. But that was before the Dirkes' time here.'

'During the war,' Henry said, 'and a year

16

or two after it. Then he went to France. And I hadn't heard a word from him since, until a couple of days ago, when I got a letter from him. . . . Surprising letter, really. Surprising offer in it. Fact is, I don't know what to think of it, but if he's serious . . . And he was a serious sort of man, shouldn't you say, Paul? Eccentric, perhaps, but perfectly serious.'

'Deadly serious,' Paul said. The thought seemed to amuse him. The little lines about his eyes deepened as he smiled. 'About coins,' he added.

'Ah,' Henry said, 'you remember the coins.'

'What else was there to remember about him?' Paul turned his head slightly, so that he looked directly at Rose. 'He came here as Henry's assistant at the Purslem during the war, when young Jackson went into the army. He was a fantastic man, about six foot three, with a perfectly grey face and piebald black and white hair, and was as nearly completely silent as it's possible for a human being to be, without being actually dumb. That was partly his difficulty with the language, I suppose. I don't think he even tried to learn English, though he lived here for about seven years. He was on a visit to England when the war broke out and he just stayed on, though he'd a wife and daughter in

Greece. But he never seemed to bother about them much. The only thing that worried him was taking care of his coin collection.'

Henry seemed troubled. 'Don't feel that's quite a fair description of him, myself—or even quite accurate. Knew him better than you did. He'd separated from his wife before the war, you see. Told me once all about her. I'd a good deal of sympathy with him. Well, that's beside the point. The point is now, he's living in Monte Carlo and he's written to me, offering to sell the Purslem his collection, and for a song.' His eyes suddenly sparkled in the dusk and he took a great gulp of whisky. 'I mean, a song!'

'But, Henry, where do Alistair and I come in?' Rose asked. 'We don't know anything about coins.'

'No,' Henry said. 'Of course not. Didn't imagine it. But it's like this. If that offer's serious, it's something we oughtn't to miss on any account whatever. I know that collection. Knew it ten years ago, when Pantelaras had already spent half a lifetime getting it together. Did it little by little, buying what he could when he could—not a rich man, you see. That's where some of the trouble came from with his wife. She didn't altogether sympathise with the way he spent his money. Don't blame her, but there it is—you can't

18

change people, and first and last he's a collector. And what a collector! The knowledge, the patience.'

'The ruthlessness,' Paul added softly.

'Who isn't ruthless at some time or other?' Henry asked with an odd sharpness. Then he moved a hand about fretfully before his face, perhaps to brush away a mosquito, perhaps a thought that had distracted him. 'Greek coins,' he went on, 'that's what he collects. Greek coins of Italy and Sicily. The masterpiece area. They're beautiful, the most beautiful—oh, yes, easily the most beautiful of Greek coins. Of any coins. Many were designed by known artists, you know, which is rare among ancient coins. Aesthetically, historically . . .' His voice died dreamily away.

After a short pause, Rose asked again, 'But where do we come in, Henry?'

'Well, if you could just go to see him,' Henry said. 'That's all. Go and see him and ask him what it's all about. There may be things he'd tell you that he wouldn't put in a letter. And you could tell him that in spite of—well, certain difficulties here, if his offer's really serious, I'll get out to see him somehow. I will. It'd be my duty.'

'Wait a minute,' Alistair said. 'Let me see if I've understood you so far, Henry. You want Rose and me to call on this man Pantelaras in Monte Carlo—'

'Or just you,' Henry said. 'Of course it doesn't have to be both of you.'

'All right,' Alistair said. 'You want one or other of us to call on this man, who's written to you, offering to sell his collection of Greek coins to the Purslem Museum for a song. By the way, just what is a song, when one's dealing in Greek coins?'

'He said he'd take six thousand pounds,' Henry said.

Paul laughed abruptly. '"A song for sixpence!"'

'The collection,' Henry said stiffly, 'is worth—well, very roughly, say, ten thousand. At least.'

'I see,' Alistair said. 'And you feel that this offer is so surprising that there's probably some catch to it—strings of some sort, perhaps, or that it's merely a feeler, when in fact he's got no serious intention of parting with his collection for that sum, or even of parting with it at all. So you want us to call on him and try to find out for you what the position is.'

'Exactly, exactly,' Henry said on a note of excitement. 'Since you're going there in any case. Since it wouldn't take you more than an hour or so. Otherwise I'd never have

20

dreamt . . . But you see how it is. The offer may be perfectly genuine, indeed probably it is. Probably he feels he has some debt of gratitude to the Purslem—something like that. Or he needs money quickly, and thinks that because of the personal connection with us and my knowledge of the collection, the deal could be put through rapidly. Oh, there are all sorts of possible explanations. And if there are, if you wrote to me and told me that in your opinion his offer was a *bona fide* one, I can tell you I should go at once. I shouldn't hesitate. It's just the fear now that . . . Well, I needn't go into all that again. You know how it is. I do need a very good reason before I undertake a journey like that.'

'And you don't want us to do anything about the coins themselves?' Alistair said.

'Not a thing,' Henry said. 'You needn't even see them.'

Alistair looked towards Rose. 'Well?' he said.

She did not answer his look or his question. Her head was tilted back and her gaze seemed to be exploring the cavity of darkness inside the foliage overhead, but he could feel, so it seemed to him, waves of resistance coming from her.

Henry, waiting humbly and hopefully, did not look at Alistair either, as if he felt that to

21

do so might be to exert an unfair pressure.

'It sounds a rather terrific responsibility,' Alistair said, irritated with Rose because she did not offer to help him in any way.

'I shouldn't mind doing it,' Paul said, 'if I were going to be in the neighbourhood. I'd rather like to see the old creature again. That great grey face of his, nodding and nodding at you, without a word coming out of him, his feet set just at forty-five degrees, his hands clasped in front of him, as if he were busy with some private prayer. . . . I'd do a portrait figure of him, I think, a genuine grotesque. Perhaps I'll try it anyhow, only I'm not much good if I can't work from the life.'

'Well, if Rose agrees . . .' Alistair said.

He had a feeling that he might not have gone as far as this if Paul had not shown so quickly that he would have been ready to do what Henry wished. But here he was wrong about himself. The issue had really been settled on the walk home, before he had even known what the issue was.

Rose gave a slight sigh, stirred in her chair and said to Henry, 'You'll want us to do it as soon as we get there, I expect.'

'Oh no,' he said. 'No, it isn't as urgent as all that. And really I ought to write to him and tell him that I'm sending someone to see him, and make sure that he agrees to the

22

scheme. He might even refuse to see anyone but me, then you'd have all your trouble for nothing. He's an odd character, I warn you, distinctly odd. So I'll do that, shall I? Write and fix up an appointment with him. No need for you to have any of that bother. Tell me when you'd like it to be, and I'll see that that's when it is.'

'Any time you like,' Alistair said. 'It won't make any difference to us.'

'You're sure? Wonderfully good of you both. Wonderfully. Can't tell you how grateful I am.' Henry stood up. 'I only hope there won't be complications.'

'Complications?' Alistair said with misgiving.

But Henry did not seem to have meant anything in particular.

'So often are, dealing with collectors,' he said. 'Queer cattle.' Then he repeated his thanks, repeated them several times, edging a few steps away towards the gate, retracing them, then edging off again, and only successfully removing himself when Paul stood up, linked an arm through him and led him away.

When they were out of earshot, Alistair picked up the whisky bottle, refilled his own glass, topped up Rose's and said, 'Sorry about that. It'll be a damn nuisance. But

23

there something about Henry . . .'

'It doesn't matter,' Rose said.

'In any case, you needn't be bothered with it. I can cope.'

He wanted to ask her why she had left the whole decision to him. He also wanted to ask her how long ago Paul had arrived, but his inability to make himself ask this second question seemed to make it impossible to ask any questions, even about the Women's Institute meeting. Curiosity of any sort seemed to threaten his own peace of mind.

'If I were Henry,' he said, 'I'd just get on a plane and go myself. Agnes would survive it.'

'If I were Agnes . . .' Rose said and stopped.

'Well?'

She sat up. There was the nervousness in her manner that he had noticed so often lately.

'If I were Agnes, I'd leave Henry, or I'd probably become a chronic invalid too,' she said.

'But I thought you quite liked him.'

'Oh, I do, but I don't have to carry the load of all his doubts and fears.' She stood up. She seemed restless now, impatient at something. There was an edge on her voice as she added, 'I wonder if he's always been the same, or if it's grown on him with time.'

24

'The general idea is that it's the result of marriage with Agnes.'

'That could be turning the problem upside down, couldn't it?'

He gave her a long look, as she stood there close to the trunk of the tree.

'I don't believe I've ever heard you say this before,' he said. 'What's made you think of it now?'

'Nothing in particular.' After a moment she added, 'This heat's beginning to get on my nerves.'

'It'll be hotter in France.'

'That'll be different.'

Alistair felt glad that in the darkness neither of their faces was clear to the other.

'Something happen to upset you this evening?' he asked.

'No,' she said. 'Why?'

'I mean, of course, at the W.I.'

'Oh! No.'

He was wishing that she would say something about Paul, some casual thing that would make his presence here seem the insignificant thing that it almost certainly had been. Almost certainly. If only she would say that they had met in the village and that she had asked him home for a drink, or else that he had dropped in a few minutes before Alistair got home, or anything whatsoever, he

25

would believe her and immediately dismiss Paul from his mind. But her silence about him was like a banging of drums, rousing detestable, barbaric emotions.

'I thought you were going to drop in at the Maybush, if you were through in time,' Alistair said.

'It felt so nice to be out here in the garden,' she answered. 'What happened at the meeting?'

'Just the usual thing. . . . No!' He slapped his knee, amazed at his own forgetfulness. 'No, something astonishing. You remember we decided last time, if possible, to get hold of some minor television notability to open the fête? Well, we've got one. Our chairman has really put his foot in it, poor man, though he doesn't know it. He's arranged for Irene Byrd to come down to do the job.'

'Irene!' Rose burst out laughing.

The sound did Alistair good, for it seemed a natural laugh, without the overtones that might have been expected, considering who Irene was.

'Oh, poor Mr. Baird,' Rose said, 'when he realises what he's done. Not that it really matters. What's a little matter of divorce among friends?'

'Except that she and Paul are capable of making horrible scenes when they meet one

26

another,' Alistair said. 'In fact, I'm wondering if it isn't the chance of making one of her awful scenes that made Irene accept the invitation. And the fête will give her lots of opportunities for doing it with the utmost publicity.'

'We'll have to have her here for the night,' Rose said, 'and keep an eye on her. Actually I think we can probably trust her. She won't really try to spoil things.'

'I hope you're right. That kind of thing can seem funny when you think about it afterwards, but it's hell at the time.'

'But I wonder why she did accept,' Rose said, turning to one of the deck-chairs and starting to fold it.

'Why do people ever accept anything?' Alistair asked. 'Why have we accepted Henry's proposition?' He added, 'Don't bother about the chairs. I'll take them in.'

'But Irene would never mind saying no, if she didn't want to do a thing,' Rose said. 'She has no conscience whatsoever.'

As she spoke, her hand moved in a light, stroking gesture along the back of the chair in which Paul Eckleston had been sitting.

Folding his own chair, Alistair somehow managed to pinch his finger in the frame, and swore violently.

27

CHAPTER THREE

Alistair's jealousy of Paul Eckleston had fluc-
tuated in intensity throughout the summer.
There were times, of which this evening was
one, when he was more vulnerable to his feelings than he was at others. He recognised this
fact, and the recognition helped to sustain his
belief that his jealousy was a functional disorder of his own nervous system, which
caused him discomfort and sometimes downright pain, but which had nothing malignant
as its cause. Perhaps his main fear regarding
it was that Rose should become aware of its
existence.

He did not believe that she was aware of it
yet. He thought that she accepted his attitude
to Paul as what he strove to make it appear;
as what, that is, it actually had been until a
certain week in the spring.

Alistair had spent that week in Holland,
at an anthropologists' conference. He had
expected Rose to accompany him, as she
often did on such occasions, but this time she
had had to stay at home, having not yet fully
recovered from an attack of 'flu. Before leaving, Alistair himself had asked Paul to keep
an eye on her, to stop her working to hard in

28

the garden before she was fit to do so, and, by dropping in from time to time, to help ward off post-'flu depression.

These things Paul had faithfully done. Rose had given Alistair an account of it all when he returned, pointing to the roses that she had managed to prune, and the beds where she had forked in a dressing of bone meal, in spite of Paul's supervision. That this account of hers had been complete and accurate in every particular, as well as given spontaneously and with pleasure, Alistair had not for a moment doubted. Yet from that time on he had sensed some change in the relationship between Rose and Paul, some alteration in the quality of their accepted friendship, some new adjustment.

For one thing, there could be no doubt now that Paul was more Rose's friend than, as had seemed to be the case before, the friend of both Rose and Alistair, equally and together.

Yet perhaps that had never been so. Alistair could not really tell, never having thought much about it until his return from Holland. If anything, he had assumed that the bond between Paul and himself was somewhat closer than that between Paul and Rose, for when the three of them had been together, most of the talk had been between the two men, and often they had gone for long walks together, Rose having made it plain that long walks were not in her line.

If Rose had seemed sometimes to possess a knowledge of Paul, of his life and his interests, that Alistair did not, he had put it down to her more observant nature and her sharper intuitions. The fact that, while he was away in London, she and Paul had always seen a certain amount of each other, had never seemed to have much significance.

Paul always appeared to have a good deal of spare time on his hands. He lived alone, his cleaning done for him by a village woman, but doing his own cooking, and he seemed on the whole to be a naturally solitary person, troubling himself about only a few friends and rarely taking part in village affairs. His house had once been the lodge of Purslem Manor, the great house that contained the famous Purslem Collection, which had been left to the county in the early nineteen twenties by the last of the Purslem family. Paul had built a studio in the garden of the lodge, into which he sometimes disappeared to work for days at a time, but he made no pretence that he lived on the returns from this activity of his. He had a private income, which he described as small, though it appeared to suffice him for the quite comfortable life that he led in the village, for frequent holidays abroad and week-ends in London.

Rose and Alistair, who had made his acquaintance very soon after they had come to live in Rollway, had already heard of him from his divorced wife, Irene. She was an old, if never very intimate friend of Rose's, one of the kind who may disappear for years at a time, at most sending Christmas cards scrawled over with affectionate messages but without addresses, then will one day walk in, without even a preliminary telephone call, with a monologue of gossip to get out of her system, some unpractical present and a host of little favours to ask. Her marriage to Paul and its dissolution had happened during one of these long absences.

On hearing that Rose and Alistair had bought a house in Rollway, she had exclaimed. 'But that's where my dear ex-husband lives! Oh, do look out, my dears. Let me tell you this, if I'd an enemy whom I wanted stabbed in the back, I couldn't do better than hand him over to Paul. Dear, gentle, quiet Paul's just great at biting the hand that feeds him. So remember you've been warned and look out!'

In his darker moods, Alistair remembered this warning of Irene's. But at the time, knowing Irene, and so more than half

31

discounting it, he had been not in the least surprised to find that Paul was a shy, pleasant, solitary man, sometimes mildly malicious in speech, but with that deep if restrained eagerness for friendship sometimes to be found in those who make a parade of liking their own company best. He seemed to be sensitive and considerate. Indeed, that this was probably the truth about him and that his tendency to treachery existed only in Irene's wifely imagination, was never quite obscured for Alistair, even in one of his dark moods.

From attacks by these, to his great relief, a few days of the holiday in France seemed to free him. As if there had never been any doubts in his mind, the image of Paul regained both its pleasantness and relative unimportance.

The weather was perfect and the lazy days on the beach, the long, slow meals out of doors, the still evenings, spent usually over a bottle of wine, in vague and drifting but delightful talk with Rose, while the scent of the pines around them deepened with the darkness, produced a state of calm in Alistair which made him realise how tense and tired he had been before their departure from England.

In Rose also he noticed a change. It was not only that her skin, already brown from her

32

days spent in the garden, took on the tawny glow that can never be bestowed by an English sun. It was not only the look of rich relaxation that came from idleness and swimming and the pleasure of eating good food, prepared by the hands of others. It was rather as if she had shed some preoccupation, had perhaps solved some problem, or come to some decision, at all events, had become free of a strain, of the force of which Alistair only became fully conscious after its disappearance.

At an earlier time in their marriage he might have made some comment on this change. In those days he and Rose had both been great believers in talking things over. But now, after fifteen years together, he did not make this demand on himself, or on her. More and more, as time passed, they had both fallen into the way of allowing a little time and a fair, unspoken understanding of one another to solve any problems that arose between them.

Rose sometimes struggled against this change. Being of the two of them by far the more inarticulate, she yet had the greater need to put her feelings into words, and a day came, about half-way through their holiday, when Alistair thought that, in spite of the peace of the last days, one of these occasions might be in preparation.

They were lying side by side on the sun-heated shingle after their first bathe of the day, when Rose suddenly raised herself on an elbow and looked fixedly into his face. His thoughts happened to be far away at the moment, and imagining dreamily that she probably wanted a cigarette, he thrust the packet towards her.

She shook her head. Her sun-glasses made blanks of her eyes, but the line of her mouth gave her face a look of concentration.

'Alistair, I've been thinking about something since we came here—there's something I want to ask you,' she said.

'Go ahead.' He retrieved the packet of cigarettes and lit one for himself. Around Rose's face her wet hair had sprung into uncontrolled little curls. She had beautiful shoulders, and long slender thighs, and it was a joy for him to watch her.

'I've been wondering, were we right to go and live at Rollway?' she asked.

It was not what he had been expecting. He looked away from her at the dazzle of light caught in the ripples on the sea's calm surface.

'Why not?' he said.

She hesitated, then said uncertainly, 'Because of you. The long journey every day.

The distance from your work.'

'I haven't complained.'

'I know.'

Alistair's gaze followed the flight of a big red rubber ball that bounced suddenly across his field of vision, with two nearly naked children chasing after it. They cannoned against each other and fell shrieking with laughter into the white foam at the water's edge.

'I like living a long way from my work,' he said. 'On the whole, it simplifies existence. People can't get at you all the time. And I don't mind the journey.'

'But something's the matter,' she said, 'even if it isn't that.'

'As a matter of fact, I like it all more than I ever expected,' he said.

'But London's in your blood.'

'And Rollway's in yours.'

'Not necessarily.'

He turned his head to look at her and found her gaze still steadily upon him through the concealing sunglasses.

'Are you really trying to say that you want to move away?' he asked.

'No,' she said, 'not at all.'

'Well then?'

'But if it's what *you* want, if it's what's been the matter with you . . .'

'Nothing's the matter with me.'

35

She lay back on the shingle, pillowing her head on a bent arm.

He repeated, 'Nothing's the matter, unless you mean the normal pressures of the summer term. They seem to get worse each year.'

'Is that all?' she asked. 'Is that really all?'

There had been a slight pause between the two questions and a cautious emphasis on the last word.

But at that moment there was a churning of shingle under two pairs of feet and Mr. and Mrs. Griffin, the only other English people staying at the same pension as the Dirkes, descended upon them, weighed down as usual by armfuls of pneumatic mattresses, beach robes, sun-tan lotions, sun-hats and Penguins. They always had so much gear with them that it made the approach of Rose and Alistair to the business of swimming and sunning themselves seem austere in its simplicity.

The Griffins now spread all these belongings on the beach not quite alongside the Dirkes, but near enough to keep up an exchange of shouted remarks about the temperature of the sea, the food at the pension, the comparative merits of the shops in Monte Carlo and in Menton and the degree of sunburn achieved by them all.

This conversation was not incessant, but to have pursued any other at the same time would have been impossible. On this occasion Alistair felt a certain gratitude to the Griffins for having arrived when they did, though, catching Rose's eye, he made a faint grimace. She did not respond to it.

That was the day, a Saturday, on which the letter came from Paul. There was also one from Henry Wallbank.

The Dirkes found them on their table on the terrace when they arrived there presently for lunch. Paul's letter was addressed to Rose, Henry's to both of them. Alistair opened Henry's letter and read it, while Rose read Paul's.

She made no comment on it. When she had finished it, she laid it down on the table between them. Her face had flushed brightly. There was a stunned, bewildered look in her eyes. She did not invite Alistair to read the letter.

If the letter had been from anyone but Paul, Alistair would, as a matter of course, have picked it up and read it without waiting to be invited to do so. For years he and Rose had shared their friends and their correspondence. But he found that he could not reach out and pick up that letter from Paul. He could hardly even bring himself to glance at

37

it, as it lay there on the table, a sheet of grey note-paper, closely covered in typing, with Paul's over-sized self-conscious signature written in red ink at the foot. He was afraid that if he did so, his expression would change too suddenly.

Instead, he handed Henry's letter to Rose.

It told them that Henry hoped that they were having a good time, said that he envied them, that Agnes had had a couple of good days, and that he hoped these would continue, as he was not really feeling too well himself; that there had been a thunderstorm and some heavy rain, but that the fine weather had returned, and that he had arranged with Mr. Pantelaras that Alistair should visit him at six-thirty on the following Friday, if this was convenient to him.

'Damn Henry! I'd been hoping he'd change his mind when he'd thought things over,' Alistair said, as he pulled the cork out of the bottle of wine on the table. 'I suppose we've got to do it.'

Rose was holding Henry's letter, looking at it, but so fixedly that Alistair did not believe that she had taken in any of it. After a moment she replied unwillingly, 'There's no way out now that I can think of.'

'And I suppose we ought to write and tell him that we'll go on Friday at six-thirty.'

'Send him and Agnes a picture postcard. I was going to do that some time anyhow.'

'Only why does one have to be bothered when one's on holiday?' He filled both their glasses, then, partly to keep his mind off Paul's letter, lying open on the table near to his hand, he went on talking. 'In a way, if it's got to be done, I wish we could do it at once and get it over. Friday's our last day but two, and it'd be much pleasanter to keep it clear. And we'll have to go into Monte Carlo in the next day or so to cash some travellers' cheques, so we might make one job of it.'

'Well, we might try ringing up Mr. Pantelaras and asking him if we could come tomorrow or the day after,' Rose suggested.

'Only my French isn't quite up to the telephone,' Alistair said.

Since Rose's French was even worse than his, she did not offer to help him out of that difficulty.

'It's nothing to worry about, in any case,' she said, and suddenly picking up Paul's letter, folded it and stuffed it into her handbag. There was an odd, bitter look in her eyes as she did so, and Alistair realised with dismay that he had just been the subject of a small but simple test.

From the next table Mrs. Griffin called out. 'Did I hear you say you were going into

Monte this afternoon? We'd love to drive you in if you are. I've told Bill I've simply got to have a go at the tables. What's the lowest amount one can stake, I wonder?'

She was a small, round person in the early sixties, with neatly waved grey hair, a gay, round, softly wrinkled face, and a liking for bright floral cotton dresses and ropes of plastic beads. Her husband was as short as she was, but lean and stringy, and, for his age, moved with a surprising degree of jerky vigour. He was a manufacturer of toys, somewhere in the Midlands. The Griffins had arrived at Cap Martin by car and were very generous with offers of lifts.

Rose and Alistair had done a little sight-seeing with them, finding it rather a strain, since Mrs. Griffin was voluble in a very exclamatory way. To-day they managed to evade the invitation, going into Monte Carlo the following day and without the Griffins, who had driven off immediately after breakfast to take a look at Nice. In the morning Rose and Alistair had had no intention of doing anything but swim and lie on the beach all day, but about midday a sharp wind sprang up, which in a very short time whipped the calm sea into a brawling mass of breakers and sent the old waiter hurrying from table to table on the terrace of the pension, clipping the check cloths on to them with clothes pegs.

By lunch-time, clouds were moving up from behind the mountains.

'Rain?' the waiter said scoffingly, when Rose questioned him. 'No, all that rain will go to Italy. When the clouds come that way, they all go to Italy.'

But he did not sound quite as convinced as he probably intended, and since the blue of the sea had changed to a harsh indigo, flecked with white, and its roar on the shingle could be heard even on the terrace, it was, Alistair suggested, a good afternoon for cashing travellers' cheques in Monte Carlo.

It was in the train that Rose made the suggestion that they should see if it was possible to call on the old coin collector that day.

'He hasn't got a telephone,' she said. 'I looked him up in the pension, after that talk we had yesterday, and there's no Pantelaras in the book. But since we're here, we could try calling. If he isn't in, or it isn't convenient, we can come again on Friday.'

'But the more I think about it, the less I like the idea of what we've got to do,' Alistair said. 'It's a hell of a responsibility.'

Perhaps for the first time it really struck him what a big responsibility his part in this deal, involving several thousand pounds, between Nikolo Pantelaras and the trustees of

41

the Purslem Collection, might turn out to be.

'I know—so it'd be nice to be done with it,' Rose said.

'All right, then, let's go.'

So when they had arrived in Monte Carlo and had cashed some travellers' cheques at Cook's, they took a taxi to the address given to them by Henry Wallbank.

The house turned out to be on the hillside above the town. At most times the spot would have been one of great beauty, with the rocky peaks rising up behind it and the shining bay spread out below. But to-day, the threatening clouds that concealed the hilltops cast a deep shadow over the town and brought out something depressingly theatrical in the scene. It was as if the brilliant lighting of clear sunshine were necessary to make the city seem itself, as a stage scene needs its special lighting to achieve the illusion of reality.

The thick mist hung not very far above the roof of the villa. It was a small, square, cream-coloured building, with the usual roof of orange-red, and with shuttered windows. There were some giant agaves and a tall date-palm in the garden, which had a high wall round it, with bougainvillæa spilling over its top in a purple cloud.

Alistair paid off the taxi and let it go before turning to the gate. It was of wrought-iron, high and narrow. Also, it was locked. But there was a bell beside it, which Alistair rang, hearing it tinkle faintly in the house.

When he and Rose had waited in the dusty road for what seemed a longer time than would have been necessary if there had been anyone in the house, he said, 'You know, coming like this could have been a bit of a mistake on our part.'

Rose was looking uneasy. 'There's something about the place . . .' she began, but did not try to finish the sentence.

'I oughtn't to have let the taxi go,' he said. 'We'll probably have to walk down again. I don't think there's anyone in.'

'Somebody's in,' she said. She was peering through the iron-work of the gate at one of the shuttered windows of the house. 'Somebody's standing at that window, looking us over.'

'Perhaps that's what you do if you keep a valuable collection of coins in the house.' He pressed the bell again. 'Let's stand here looking very harmless. And if we have to identify ourselves formally as Henry's envoys, we can always produce our passports.'

'I'm afraid it probably *was* a mistake to come,' Rose said. 'I'm sorry I suggested it.' But just then the door of the house opened and an extraordinary figure advanced

43

towards the gate.

He was as Paul Eckleston had described Nikolo Pantelaras. He was a very tall man, but except for his height, he was small in every particular, his hands, his feet, his head, all except the great grey face that hung like a mask, fantastically topped by piebald black and white hair, between his little shoulders. He looked so dry and fragile that he could have been crumpled like a roll of paper between a pair of hands. He was wearing a pale grey suit, very trimly pressed, and grey suede shoes with thick rubber soles, which made his approach to the gate quite noiseless.

Reaching it, he stood still inside it, his hands clasped together, his body inclined slightly forwards, so that he would have appeared to be making an almost obsequious bow, if the way that his head was bent to regard first Alistair, and then Rose, had not implied a suspicious challenge.

He waited for them to speak.

Alistair began in French, explaining who he and Rose were and why they had come that day. But he was humble about his foreign languages and when he saw no trace of response on the face that peered at them so strangely through the iron gate, like that of a prisoner, pale and empty from years of captivity, he switched to English.

That also produced no response. It made Alistair wonder if perhaps he ought to try shouting, in case deafness were the explanation of the old man's apparent failure to understand him.

But just as he was about to turn to Rose to see what she was making of the situation, Nikolo Pantelaras spoke.

'Friday,' he said in a low, husky voice. 'Friday, six-thirty.'

'Then to-day's inconvenient?' Alistair said. 'In that case, I'm sorry to have troubled you.'

There was a little pause, then the old man spoke again. 'All is arranged for Friday. Thank you.'

'Yes,' Alistair said helplessly. 'Certainly. Friday. Good afternoon.'

He put his hand on Rose's arm and was drawing her away from the gate when the collector spoke once more.

'To-day nothing is here. On Friday I go to the bank.'

Alistair thought that he saw light. Mr. Pantelaras imagined that he had to produce his collection, normally kept in the bank, for Rose and Alistair to see. He had not really comprehended Henry's reasons for sending them to call on him.

'But there's no need for that,' Alistair had begun, when he realised that Rose was tugging at his hand, urging him to come away.

Muttering some more apologies, which Rose echoed, he went with her down the road. For a moment neither of them spoke. Then, when it was certain that they were out of earshot of the tall figure, which, for all that they knew, might still be watching them through the iron bars of the gate, Alistair said, 'That most certainly was a mistake!'

'I'm so sorry,' Rose said. 'I'm so sorry I ever suggested it.'

'On the whole I'm glad you did,' he said. 'Now we know what we're in for.'

'You aren't going back,' she said.

'I've got to, haven't I?'

'No, you can write and tell Henry it's quite impossible.'

'Only that would be letting him down pretty badly.'

'But he was such a horrible man—quite horrible. Sinister.'

Her intense seriousness made Alistair laugh. He remembered what Henry had said about Nikolo Pantelaras.

'Just an eccentric,' he said. 'Not a very prepossessing one, at first sight, but perhaps he'll improve on acquaintance.'

'You really mean you're going on with it?'

'Well, what else can I do? You needn't come again, if you don't want to. In fact, that might be best. I think it's easier to be without an audience when one's trying to communicate with a jibbering lunatic—though of course, he didn't exactly jibber.'

'I should think he might start when he produces his beloved coins,' she said. 'And that's one of the things that's worrying me. Why's he producing them?—if that's what he meant about going to the bank.'

'He may not have understood Henry, or he may just like showing off his treasures.'

'Or did it all mean something else?'

'Now, listen—'

'All right, all right!' Her voice went up sharply. 'Let's not go on talking about it. Let's—let's go and have some tea at that place where they have the gorgeous cakes.'

She started to hurry, as if she wanted to put as much space as she could between themselves and the old man in the villa.

Their hurrying did not save them from a wetting before they reached their favourite *patisserie*. The rain came suddenly out of the low clouds. It came in great warm drops that struck the ground with a rattle which made Alistair think, as he and Rose ran for the shelter of an awning over a shop-window, of a handful of coins being dropped all over the pavement.

Waiting for the shower to end, he caught

himself sketching in his imagination a shockingly melodramatic picture of Nikolo Pantelaras, standing slightly bent forward and with his hands together, rubbing them in a miser's gesture of gloating, while his dark, cold eyes reflected brilliantly a heap of coins before him.

Greek coins, Alistair remembered. Were they gold, he wondered, or silver, or what? It was preposterous to be going on a mission like this, knowing so little of what he was up to. But he recognised that it was too late to withdraw, and later in the afternoon, when they had had tea and were on their way back to the station, they stopped at a stall to buy a picture postcard to send to Henry to tell him that they would call on Mr. Pantelaras on the following Friday.

Rose made the purchase while Alistair was choosing a newspaper, and it was she who wrote and posted the card while they were waiting for their train. She had said nothing about wanting to post any other card or letter, yet as her hand went out to the neat little grey Monaco letter-box, Alistair saw that she held not only the card for Henry, but another as well.

Alistair did not say anything about it. He could not have said anything, any more than he had been able, the day before, to pick up

48

and read Paul Eckleston's letter. But for several hours after that moment, he forgot all about Nikolo Pantelaras, as he also forgot the pleasantness and peace of the time that he and Rose had spent at Cap Martin together.

CHAPTER FOUR

At that time the following Friday still seemed fairly distant. So did the journey home and the return to normal existence. But as the end of the holiday approached, time seemed to accelerate and suddenly Friday, with its problems, was there.

In the morning, Rose and Alistair had an argument about their plans for the day, but in the end Rose gave way and let Alistair go by himself to Monte Carlo. He knew that she had had no real reluctance to do this, but had believed that she ought not to try to escape an unpleasant duty. In reality, he had decided that he would far prefer to handle the collector alone.

He took an afternoon train, arriving in Monte Carlo with nearly an hour to fill in before he could call at the villa. He began by strolling down to the harbour, looking at the yachts and wondering how, with income tax what it was in Britain, and with currency allowances at a hundred pounds, some of those flying the British flag managed to keep afloat.

Perhaps, he thought, this was a question with which, as a social anthropologist, he ought to concern himself, though he suspected that it would remain for ever beyond his intellectual grasp. In any case, the little harbour was a charming sight. Climbing up into the town again, and finding that he had still some time to spare, he paid his two hundred francs and went into the Casino, into which he had not been since before the war, in spite of the fact that he and Rose had spent their summer holidays, for several years running, at Cap Martin.

He stayed in the Casino for about a quarter of an hour. It amused him, while he was in the great room that brings to mind so vividly the architecture of the Euston Hotel, to see Mr. Griffin sitting at one of the tables, with his wife, in a red, yellow and green floral cotton dress and three ropes of yellow plastic beads, standing behind him. There was something about Mr. Griffin, about his tense posture and the rigid, empty look on his face, that was rather surprising, making Alistair wonder whether a very little encouragement might not turn the manufacturer of toys from the Midlands into a small but avid and uncontrollable gambler. Emerging, Alistair looked for a taxi.

On arriving at the villa on the hillside, he dismissed it, having no doubts of the wisdom of this to-day. Nikolo Pantelaras was not the man to miss an appointment. Perhaps he would refuse to admit a caller five minutes before the agreed time, and perhaps hold it seriously against him if he arrived five minutes after it. But the punctual caller could rely on his presence. Or so Alistair took for granted until he had rung the bell at the gate three times and had received no answer. At that point he became worried.

It occurred to him only then to try the gate. It was unlocked. That surprised him and for a moment only sharpened the worry. Then he thought that perhaps the gate had been left unlocked simply because he was expected. Or perhaps the bell was out of order, making it necessary to leave the gate unlocked.

All sorts of explanations were possible, so many, indeed, that as he walked up the gravel path and mounted the stone steps to the house, Alistair forgot that he had had that first irrational reaction of dread.

He forgot it until he had rung the bell inside the door several times and still received no answer.

Even then, he reasoned with himself, it was ridiculous to leap to the conclusion that anything was seriously wrong. But there are times when the mind insists on working with uncontrollable swiftness, putting two and two together with preposterous logic. Between the third and fourth times that he had rung the bell and had heard it clang noisily inside the house, he had remembered the locked gate of the earlier afternoon, the nervous old man behind it, and the valuable collection of coins that presumably had been brought from the bank that day. *A collection which possibly a number of people knew had been brought from the bank that day.*

But then, naturally, came reasonable explanations for the collector's failure to answer the bell. For instance, he was a frail old man, and might suddenly have been taken ill and been fetched away in an ambulance. The ambulance men would probably not have remembered to lock the gate after them. Or perhaps the idea of him as a man of excessively precise and punctual habits was totally mistaken, and he had simply forgotten all about the appointment and gone out for a walk by himself. And so on.

All the same, what did one do about it?

Alistair had dismissed the first violent images that had come to his mind and was deciding that if, when he rang the bell once more, there was still no answer, he would go back to the station, take the next train back to Cap Martin and dismiss the whole matter from his mind, when he heard a footstep on the gravel below him, and turning, saw, just inside the gate, a young woman.

She spoke at once, sharply, suspiciously. 'Who are you? How did you get in?'

Questions, thought Alistair, about which there were one or two peculiar things. They were not, to begin with, courteous. Secondly, they were in English, which suggested that in fact she knew perfectly well who he was.

This second point was emphasised for him by the fact that his very first thought about her was that he had seen her before. He had no idea where or when, but the feeling that her small dark face with its bright, dimpled cheeks, wide across the cheek-bones, its wide dark eyes and black curly hair, was familiar, startled and confused him for a moment.

She looked about twenty-eight years old, was of medium height, with a very small waist and small hands and feet, but was formed in general with a delicate and charming plumpness. Her yellow sun-dress revealed soft shoulders, tanned to a rich and even brown.

Could she—this was the question that Alistair always asked himself first, when he had this feeling of having seen a person before—could she possibly once have been a student of his? Take away seven or eight years, take away the curves . . .

Before he could arrive at an answer, she had repeated, 'I said, how did you get in?'

'By the gate,' he answered.

'It was open?' There was a very faint foreign accent in her speech. She sounded disbelieving.

'It was unlocked,' Alistair said. 'As a matter of fact, I was a little surprised myself, but thought it was probably because I was expected.'

'Ah, so you *are* the professor.'

She made the word sound extraordinarily sinister, as if in her mind it conjured up an image of Professor Moriarty, or one of his literary descendants.

'I'm Professor Dirke,' Alistair said, in case there should be any mistake. 'I had an appointment with Mr. Pantelaras at six-thirty.'

'I know,' she said. 'I know all about it—all.'

'I wish I did,' he said.

She came forward. 'You have rung the bell? You have rung and nobody answers?'

Without waiting for his reply, she put her finger on the bell and held it there, listening as it shrilled inside the house. Then, fixing her big dark eyes on Alistair's face, she gazed at him as if she were challenging him not to produce immediately some answer to that long peal. But when there was still no sound inside the house, she looked as if she were forgetting her suspicions in her own growing dismay.

'I don't understand it,' she said after a moment.

'Then you think something's wrong?' Alistair said. 'I wasn't sure. I had the appointment, but I thought perhaps Mr. Pantelaras might have forgotten it.'

'Impossible,' she said. 'My father would never . . .' She paused. 'I beg your pardon, I haven't told you that I am Madame Robinet. And I came here on purpose to see you and to implore you not to let my father do this thing. This cruel and wicked thing. Believe me, I have suffered enough already.'

Alistair's long academic experience had given him a certain ease in producing an air of bright but non-committal interest when he had no idea what another person was talking about.

'Do you think perhaps Mr. Pantelaras may have been taken ill?' he asked.

'In that case, why should the gate be unlocked?'

'Yes, I see the point. Then perhaps we ought to take a look round.'

'I think so. I think something must have happened to him.'

'Don't you think he may simply have forgotten the whole thing?'

'When he has nothing else to think about?' Her face had become rigid with anxiety.

Recalling his own first thoughts when there had been no answer to his ringing, Alistair saw nothing surprising in this, but afterwards he wondered if there had not been something strange about the fact that she had shown quite so much anxiety so quickly.

'Well, where do we start?' he asked. 'I suppose you haven't a key to the house?'

'The door is locked?' she asked swiftly. 'You have tried it?'

'Why, no. I just took for granted that it was locked.'

'If the gate is open, then perhaps the door too. . . .' She put a hand out to the door-knob, turned it and pushed. The door swung open.

At this point several things occurred to Alistair in swift succession.

The first was that he had no proof at all that the young woman was the daughter of Nikolo Pantelaras. The second was that to walk into the house now with her, simply because the door was unlocked, might easily be construed as illegal entry. The third was that he ought to have thought of these things a little sooner. The fourth was that, short of

57

pulling the girl backwards onto the doorstep and demanding further explanations, there was not much he could do but follow her inside.

Calling himself all kinds of a fool, he stepped into the shadowy hall, just as the girl, stepping swiftly backwards, flung up an arm over her eyes with a scream that pierced the shadows like a jagged flash of light.

As she bumped into Alistair the door-knob was jerked from his hand and the door closed behind him with a loud slam. Then there was utter silence, as the two of them stared down at the grotesque and terrible figure of Nikolo Pantelaras, sprawled on the ground at their feet, with his head battered in.

CHAPTER FIVE

It was many hours later that Alistair, in a taxi, arrived back at the pension at Cap Martin.

At some time during that nightmarish evening he had managed to telephone Rose, and he found her waiting up for him in their room, still dressed, as if she had half-expected to be called out at any moment. She was holding a book open on her knee, but the feverish light in her eyes made it seem unlikely that she had really been reading. As she sprang to her feet and ran to Alistair, the book fell to the floor, face downwards, its pages doubling up in disorder.

That was the kind of thing that Alistair always automatically set right. When Rose released him, he bent and picked up the book.

'God, what an evening!' He laid the book down on the table, saw the heap of her cigarette stubs in the ashtray, then suddenly felt that he had to clutch at her and say in her ear, 'I'm sorry, I'm sorry.'

It was for their shattered peace that he was sorry, and for the fact that, weeks ago, at the parting of the ways, because of a reasonless distrust of her, he had pressed Henry Wallbank to come home with him for a drink.

Poor old Henry, who had done this to them, though no one could possibly blame him for it.

'Have you had anything to eat?' Rose asked, a blessed question which steadied him by making him want to laugh.

'Yes, something,' he said.

There had been coffee somewhere, he remembered, with that dark-eyed girl and her husband, who had appeared during the evening, and for some reason had been given a worse time than any of them by the police, which was something, Alistair realised, that the girl had expected.

As soon as he had appeared, a tall fair young man with a sharp-featured face that seemed mobile and eager, yet was in fact extraordinarily expressionless, she had become very quiet. All the hysteria that had burst out of her at the start had vanished. The dark eyes had become guarded and watchful.

'I've got a hell of a headache,' Alistair said.

Rose fetched the aspirins and a glass of water.

When he had swallowed two tablets and gulped down the water, she took the glass from him, refilled it and drank avidly herself. Then she picked up a comb and pulled it fiercely through her hair. He saw that her forehead was wet with sweat.

'I wanted to come,' she said. 'Why didn't you let me?'

He shook his head confusedly, and taking off his jacket, threw it down on a chair, kicked off his shoes and slumped down on the edge of the bed. The room was very hot, though the two tall windows behind the wire screens were wide open above the sea.

'It isn't all over yet, you know,' he said. 'God knows what we're in for.'

'Tell me how it was,' she said.

'Well, it's as I told you when I telephoned.'

'You didn't say much when you telephoned.'

'Didn't I?' He was conscious of an immense amount to say and a great need to say it, and of the almost insuperable difficulty of saying anything at all. 'Someone had broken in—that's to say, got in. There weren't any signs of breaking in. Someone had been let in by Pantelaras himself, that's how they think it was, and bashed the poor devil's skull in with a brass door-stop, and stolen his collection. His damned collection.'

'Do they know. . . ?'

'Who did it? They seem to be gunning for the son-in-law, though I don't know why, except that he and Pantelaras weren't on

61

speaking terms.'

'You mean they've arrested him?'

'No, they haven't arrested anybody.'

'What were they like, the police?'

'All right. Just doing their jobs.'

'Somehow it's hard to take them seriously in their pretty grey uniforms,' she said.

'They weren't the ones in the pretty grey uniforms. Those are the Monacan police. When something like this happens, the French police come in. There was a fat sallow man in a tight brown suit. . . . We'll see some more of him to-morrow, I think.'

'But they can't think that you're mixed up in this!'

He gave his aching head a shake.

Her tone sharpened. *'Do* they?'

'No, I don't think so,' he said. 'But I got there first. I was there on the doorstep already when the girl turned up. No one saw me try the gate and find it unlocked, and the girl kept reminding them of that. I don't know if that's going to mean trouble.'

'The girl?' Rose asked.

'Didn't I tell you about her? Madame Robinet, the daughter.'

'You've hardly told me anything.'

He nodded, realising that of course this was so, that he had done no more than bark a few bald facts at her.

'Well, it began,' he said, 'with my getting no answer when I rang the bell at the gate, and then finding that it wasn't locked.'

From there he went on to tell her of his ringing of the door-bell, of the arrival of the girl, of their entry together and discovery of the body.

Rose came and sat down beside him on the bed while he was talking, and, propping herself against the pillows, pulling her feet up under her, kept a steady gaze on his face. Her closeness calmed him and he reached out and took her hand.

'She began by going to pieces completely,' he said. 'Screamed and cried and nearly fainted. Then all of a sudden she pulled herself together and rushed into one of the rooms where there was a safe. It was standing wide open and there wasn't a thing in it. Then she became perfectly calm and said that we must call the police at once. There wasn't a telephone in the house, so I didn't know quite how to set about it, but she said that there was one in the house next door and that she'd go and do it. I didn't know which was the better thing to do, to let her go and perhaps vanish into thin air, or to go myself and leave her to get up to God knows what in the house. And she seemed to be having the same doubts about me, but I believe she wanted,

63

beyond anything else, to ring up her husband. While she was gone, I had a quick look round the place.'

He raised his head and smiled at her.

'Ever thought of renting a villa on the Riviera?' he asked. 'There's one that'll be going now, all musty plush and the sort of furniture that looks as if it must have been hacked out by a monumental mason, and all looking and smelling as if the sun hadn't been allowed inside for half a century. It didn't tell me much except that whoever it was that had come in and done the murder, must have been let in by Pantelaras himself or had a key. All the shutters were shut tight and most of the windows. The police said the same later, and everyone agreed it meant that the murderer was someone Pantelaras knew, or at least had been expecting.'

'Expecting!'

'Yes.'

'And the girl, did she come back?'

'Yes, almost at once, with a whole mass of neighbours, and they trampled all around the place, all talking together. Then the police turned up and did a good deal of trampling too and a good deal of talking, even before the questions got properly started. And then the questions! Who I was, and what I was doing there, and so on. Naturally. But somehow it didn't seem just the easiest thing in the world to explain, though in the end I believe they got it fairly clear. The point that was hardest to get over was why, if I hadn't come there to look at the coins, Pantelaras should have got them out of the bank that day to show me. All I could suggest was that he enjoyed showing them off to anyone who'd look at them, or else that he hadn't understood Henry's letter. Or else . . .'

'Well?' she said.

'Well, I didn't actually think of it till I'd left, but suppose he hadn't got them out to show to me. I mean, suppose that he was expecting someone else before me. Suppose that I, or rather Henry, wasn't the only bidder in the field.'

She exclaimed, 'That must be it! Because that makes sense of what happened the other day. If he didn't want to talk to you until he'd talked to this other person, of course he wouldn't let us in.'

'I know, but there are one or two difficulties about that.'

'What are they?'

'Mainly the preposterously low price he'd asked the Purslem. If you're playing two bidders off against one another, you don't begin by asking much less than you mean to get in the end.'

65

'Don't you? I suppose not.' Then she caught at his arm. 'You might! You might, if you never had any intention of selling to the person from whom you were asking the low price.'

'Why make the offer, then?'

'Just to get the person to come to see you. To make sure he'd have to take an interest and come—and come quickly.'

'Because in fact there wasn't a second bidder?'

'Something like that.'

'I suppose it's possible,' he said uncertainly, trying to think it out further, but distracted by the throbbing in his head.

Rose leant back again against the pillows. 'Poor old Henry. He was so thrilled at the chance to get his hands on that collection.'

'But if it was as good as he seemed to think, surely there would have been other bidders,' Alistair said.

'Perhaps it would have taken time to find them.'

'Time,' Alistair said. 'I wonder if that's the answer. If Pantelaras wanted money immediately, if he'd had an offer and wanted to push it up, if he thought that a dummy bidder on the spot might help. . . . Only that doesn't really fit with what his daughter told me.'

'What did she tell you?'

66

'That he was giving the collection away to spite her. She said he hated her husband and hadn't forgiven her for marrying him. She came that afternoon, so she said, on purpose to speak to me and implore me not to let her father go ahead with his scheme. She didn't know, of course, that I'd no power in the matter. She thought I was the Purslem's accredited representative and might almost be planning to walk off with the collection under my arm. Apparently that's what he'd told her. And since he'd nothing else of value to leave her, it was his way of disinheriting her.'

'He was asking six thousand pounds for it, wasn't he?' Rose said. 'That isn't exactly a gift.'

'Perhaps that's how you regard it if you know it's worth much more,' he said.

'What did you think of her?' she asked. 'Did you believe what she told you?'

'You mean, do I think she could be involved in the murder?'

'Yes.'

'I'm not sure,' he said. 'She didn't seem to have any affection for her father. The scene she made when she nearly tripped over his body seemed to me just a case of shock at the sight. As I said, she recovered remarkably fast when she remembered that the collection was supposed to be in the house. All the same, I don't think I'd blame her too much for that. I doubt if he was a lovable father.'

'What about her mother? Is she still alive?'

'Yes, but divorced and married again, so she was out of the running for the money anyway. Incidentally, the mother's English, which explains why the daughter speaks the language so well. And that reminds me, there was something about her that puzzled me at first. I felt absolutely certain that I'd seen her before. You know the feeling. You can get it sometimes even when you know you couldn't possibly ever have seen the person. I had it the moment she appeared at the gate.'

'And where had you seen her?'

'Oh, I hadn't—I'm sure of that now.'

'But you said it puzzled you *at first*—as if you'd solved it later on.'

'I didn't mean that. I meant that I only had the *feeling* at first. It disappeared as soon as I'd been talking to her for a little while.' He stood up, giving his arms a weary stretch. 'Well, I suppose we may as well go to bed, though I don't suppose we'll sleep much.'

Rose did not move. Her gaze followed him absently as he started to wander about the room, undressing.

After a moment she asked, 'Have you sent any message about all this to Henry?'

'Not yet,' he said. 'We'd better send off a long telegram to-morrow. He may think he ought to come out.'

'Not Henry,' she said. 'Not if he can help it. Henry likes to avoid trouble. But we'll be stuck here, shan't we?'

'Well, it isn't a bad place to be stuck.'

She made no answer, and Alistair, glancing at her because of her silence, surprised on her face a hard frown. But as soon as she realised that his eyes were on her, the frown faded, leaving her face as calmly empty as if it had just been deliberately wiped clear of all expression. Standing up, she started to undress too, with tired, preoccupied movements.

Neither of them slept much that night. Stirring from time to time, each knowing that the other was awake, they spoke a little, Alistair remembering details that he had left out before, when he had been describing what had taken place in the villa in Monte Carlo, Rose asking an occasional question.

As recurrent as some of the questions in both their minds, even when it seemed that they had found a reasonable answer, a mosquito kept buzzing about their pillows, its threatening little *ping* rousing one or other just when there seemed some hope of drifting off to sleep. Alistair waved a fretful hand at it

69

and cursed it, but again and again it returned to the attack. The sound of the surf on the beach seemed so loud that the sea, he thought, must still be stormy.

Yet in the morning, when he got up and went out on to the narrow balcony that stretched between the two windows, he saw both sea and sky drenched in bright sunshine, meeting in a blue calm at the hazy horizon. The savage breakers that he had heard in the night had grown still very suddenly, or else all the time had owed most of their thunder to his imagination.

It would not have been difficult, in that morning freshness, to convince himself that the events of the previous evening had been part of a nightmare, but he was not given much opportunity to indulge this attractive delusion. The maid, who brought in their coffee, knew of the murder, and that in some way Alistair was connected with it, and breathed her horror and excitement at him in gasping little explosions of the local dialect, which it was beyond him to interpret. When presently he and Rose went downstairs, other visitors at the pension greeted them with an unusual degree of warmth and interest. People whom they did not even know were staying in the pension seemed to be claiming old acquaintance with them.

Only Mr. and Mrs. Griffin were missing. The old waiter, raking the gravel on the terrace, remarked on this fact with a good deal of significant shoulder shrugging and eyebrow raising.

'They left last night,' he said. 'To go on into Italy. Suddenly they have a passion to go on into Italy.'

As he wandered off, Rose said with a sigh, 'Well, I don't blame them. A murder isn't the most cheering thing to have happen on a holiday.'

'If they left last night,' Alistair said, 'it can't have had anything to do with the murder, because they can't have heard about it.' He gave a sudden laugh. 'Do you know why I think they've gone? I think they got cleaned out at the Casino.'

'What do you mean?'

He started to tell her of the glimpse that he had had of the Griffins in the Casino, but broke off as he realised that the strange look of apprehension that had come to Rose's face had nothing to do with the Griffins. With her head tilted slightly on one side, she was listening intently, but not to him.

Listening too, Alistair heard voices, one the old waiter's, the other, harsh and official, a voice that Alistair regretfully recognised. They came from the steps, out of sight round

71

a corner of the house, that led up from the terrace to the roadway.

As Rose raised her eyes to him with an anxious question in them, he nodded.

'Yes, that's the man,' he said. 'The one who seemed to be in charge.'

'Oh, why can't they leave us alone?' she said under her breath.

'Well, let's hope this is the end of it,' he said. 'I've already told them every damn' thing I could think of.'

'But why did this have to happen to us? When we came away there was only one thing I wanted—and I wanted it so badly. I wanted to be with you, just alone with you.'

The violence in her tone and in the look she gave him as she said it gave Alistair a shock. It sounded almost as if she were accusing him of something, and doing it with a sort of hatred.

He slipped a hand through her arm.

'But there's nothing to worry about,' he said, rather helplessly.

'Who's worrying?' she muttered with a rough mockery in her voice that did not sound at all like her.

'All right, then, we're both worrying,' he said. 'But we're fools.'

'We were fools not to do what the Griffins have done.'

'For God's sake, Rose . . .'

She drew a long breath. 'I'm sorry. I seem to be behaving badly. Of course we couldn't leave. I didn't mean it. But I meant what I said before. . . .'

She did not finish, because that was the moment when the fat sallow man in the tight brown suit appeared round the corner of the house.

He was a tall man, besides being a fat one, a man built on a scale quite different from the normal, with hands and feet and head all bigger than such objects generally are, so that each was something to divert the attention from the commonplace plump face with the small sharp eyes.

Moving with short steps, quick, impatient and uneven, as if the burden of his bulk were a little too much for him, he came up to Rose and Alistair, holding out one of his great hands and smiling such an eager wide smile that it seemed certain that Alistair had been right in saying that he and Rose had nothing to worry about. Looming over them, the fat man's whole bowing, perspiring presence was an admonition to them not to worry.

'It's convenient if we talk for a little?' he said. 'I hope so. I hope you have a few minutes to spare. And you'll join me in a glass of wine, perhaps. I haven't yet breakfasted. A

73

long night . . . Thank you,' as Alistair placed a chair for him. 'I've already given the order. I have to eat when I can. Yes, a long night, but I felt it my duty to inform you, since you were so unfortunately caught up in the unpleasant circumstances, that the matter is, as I know you and madame will be relieved to hear, to all intents and purposes, closed.'

'You mean you've arrested the murderer already?' Alistair said.

'Yes, we have made an arrest,' the fat man said. 'But first let me tell you that we've found confirmation, complete confirmation, of what you told us last night. A letter. We found a letter from Monsieur Wallbank, Director of the Purslem Collection, in the bureau in the living-room, addressed to Monsieur Pantelaras. It contains just what you told us. A statement that you would be calling on Monsieur Pantelaras to inquire into certain matters connected with the proposed sale of his collection. It adds that your lack of numismatics is unimportant, since the collection is already well known to Monsieur Wallbank. It covers the situation most perfectly. It removes entirely all doubt.'

'Doubt?' Alistair said.

'Of the reason for your presence on the scene. Knowing nothing of you, we are, naturally, compelled to doubt what you tell us.'

After only a faint hesitation, Alistair said, 'Naturally.'

'Though if, as at first sight did not, I must confess, seem wholly improbable, you had had some connection with the event,' the fat man went on, 'if, in fact, Madame Robinet had surprised you, not in the act of attempting to enter the house, but of leaving it, the question would still have remained, what had you done with the coins? Where were they? Where *are* they?'

'Just for the record,' Alistair said, 'I wasn't attempting to enter the house. I was merely standing there, wondering what to do next.'

'Please,' Rose put in at that point, 'whom have you arrested?'

The huge head turned towards her and the little eyes glinted above the thick yellow cheeks.

'We're arrested Robinet, madame. The son-in-law. But to return to the collection. . . . Ah, my breakfast.'

The waiter had come out of the house with a tray on which were a bottle of wine, glasses, a plate of salami and half a loaf of bread.

The detective repeated his invitation to Rose and Alistair to drink a glass of wine with him, but when, unable to face it at that time of the morning, they declined, he went on, 'To return to the collection. That remains the

75

problem. Robinet refuses to tell us where he concealed it. His wife, if she knows where it is, also refuses. But I'm not sure that she knows. Her fear that the coins have been stolen and that she may never see them again appears to me perfectly genuine. There is also the question of the gun.'

'The gun?'

'Both Robinets maintain that Monsieur Pantelaras kept a gun in the house to protect himself. If so, it was stolen along with the coins. But perhaps in reality there was no gun.'

'I talked to Robinet last night,' Alistair said thoughtfully. 'He seemed a quite pleasant man.'

'Ah, a smooth type,' the detective said. 'Intelligent, charming. The woman adores him and will do all she can to defend him. You saw that when she tried so hard to implicate you, monsieur.'

'It's possible she really believed I was the murderer,' Alistair said.

'Of course she believes it,' the fat man said. 'Naturally she believes it.' He munched a mouthful of bread and salami. 'We believe what we wish to believe.'

Rose shifted her gaze from his face to Alistair's. As she continued to look at him, she might have been trying, perhaps not very successfully, to see in him the man whom another woman had succeeded in suspecting of murder. He gave her a faint smile and turned back to the detective. 'Is there evidence against Robinet, apart from his quarrel with his father-in-law?'

Munching and swallowing, the fat man nodded.

'There is evidence. He was seen leaving the house not half an hour before you arrived there. He was seen by reliable witnesses, a father and daughter, who live in the neighbourhood and were out for a walk together. And his fingerprints are in the house, though he denies having been inside it.'

'He denies it all, then?'

'So far. But he'll change his story soon. Soon he'll admit he went to the house, will say he found the door unlocked, went in and found his father-in-law already dead. And there will be a mysterious stranger whom he saw coming away. That will be the only thing for him to say. And he'll continue to deny all knowledge of the coins.'

'And what *has* happened to the coins?'

The immense shoulders sketched a shrug.

'They may be out of the country already. That's a probability. We're very near the Italian frontier.'

'And they'll never be heard of again?'

'Perhaps, perhaps not.'

'Anyway, not by Henry,' Rose murmured. 'Can you tell us, monsieur, whether you'll need my husband any more? Our holiday ends this week. We'd intended to leave for home on Sunday. Are we free to leave?'

'Of course, of course, that's why I hurried here to see you, to tell you not to concern yourselves any more, to enjoy the rest of your holiday, to go home when you will. It may be that Monsieur Dirke will be required later to give evidence. I think this quite likely. But meanwhile there is no reason why you should not go home.'

She gave him a dim but relieved smile, then turned and looked out at the sea.

Alistair also felt a great relief. There had been very few occasions when the thought of the small Georgian house in Rollway, with its pretty garden and the cherry tree that cast its shade over the lawn, had seemed quite as attractive as it did at that moment. Yet when the detective observed that no doubt they would find their home very peaceful after this, Alistair saw Rose's lips contract as if she were biting back a swift rejoinder, while a look of apprehension darkened her eyes, and it came to him with sharp certainty that that statement of the detective's was not the most accurate that he had made that morning.

78

CHAPTER SIX

Peacefulness, for one thing, was never the state that prevailed in Rollway, even when there was no spreading suspicion there of something more serious than the normal misdemeanours of village life, during the last week before the annual fête and flower show.

But when Rose and Alistair first returned, the only suspicion that seemed to be abroad in the village was that a certain Mr. Tolliver, who was entering spring-sown onions at the show, had in fact no onions in his garden. Since there was a ten-foot wall round his garden, it was difficult to investigate the truth of the rumour, but there was no doubt that on the previous Saturday, at the auction held at the end of the show in a neighbouring village, Mr. Tolliver had been seen buying the prize-winning onions. This was thought to be a sinister circumstance.

One other complication had arisen in connection with the Rollway show. Some sort of platform, naturally, was necessary for Irene Byrd to stand on when she made her speech, and it had been assumed by the committee that a certain farmer would loan his trailer for the purpose. But this he had flatly refused to do, on the grounds that his trailer had rubber tyres and that when the young of South Rollway arrived at the show, with knives in their pockets and heaven knew what in their heads, only a vehicle with steel treads could be considered suitable. Alistair, consulted, suggested that it might be possible to borrow an armoured car from the nearest American camp.

He found problems such as these very calming to nerves that were a good deal more frayed than they should have been at the end of a holiday.

He had sent Henry a long telegram from Cap Martin on the day after the murder. He had had no reply to it, but within a few minutes of his arrival home with Rose, Henry had telephoned, saying that he had been telephoning at half-hour intervals all that day, and being very insistent that he and Alistair should meet that evening. They had arranged that Alistair should drop in at the Wallbanks' house about eight-thirty.

The Wallbanks lived in a house on the Purslem estate. To reach it by the shortest way from his home, Alistair had to pass the lodge where Paul Eckleston lived, walk a little way towards the manor-house along a beautiful avenue of beeches, then turn off it down a path that led across a smooth sweep of the park to what appeared to be a dense clump of trees, but which had in its centre a small, curiously cheerless and uncomfortable house.

It was a house disliked by both Wallbanks, but because it went with Henry's job as Director of the Purslem Collection and was rent free, they had never considered moving away from it. Nor, it seemed, had they ever considered improving it in any way.

Alistair had always felt sorry for Henry for having to live in that house, yet for most of its dreariness he blamed Agnes. For even if the windows were small and shadowed by dank bushes, the fireplaces ugly and inadequate, the paintwork and wallpapers drab, and even if the money that might have been used for beautifying it a little had had to be used for Agnes's frequent operations, the rooms, Alistair thought, need not all have looked so bleakly like those of the cleanest but unfriendliest type of boarding-house. It was unimaginable to him that Henry, who loved and understood beautiful objects, and who lived among them and cared for them all day, should do anything but suffer horribly when he had to return at night to all that linoleum, that shoddy fumed oak and those shiny leather cushions. If only there had been a few books lying around, or a few flowers in a vase, they might have helped to take the chill off the grim little rooms, but such things would have offended Agnes's sense of rigid tidiness.

Yet Agnes, in herself, was not a tidy woman. Her grey hair straggled in wisps about her face, her stockings were always in wrinkles, her knitted jumpers were usually frayed at the cuffs. She was very thin and her clothes hung on her as if they belonged to somebody else. Even her shoes, which she always forgot to have mended when they needed it, looked as if they were several sizes too large for her. That she might once have had a certain delicate and shy attraction was suggested by a photograph of her, in one of the short wedding dresses of the twenties, that stood on the well-polished but mute piano. But in the pale, brooding face with the eyes that seemed either lifeless or lit up by the gleam of nervous excitement, which was the only face that Rollway had ever seen on her, there was nothing to recall that all too destructible kind of charm.

She spent her time in frenzies of house-work which alternated with long periods of resting, would hardly ever leave the house and, though she always accepted any invitation that came to her, would at the last moment generally find some reason why she could not possibly go out. Only at times, alone with one other person, so Rose had told Alistair, she would suddenly forget her aches and pains, her anxieties and grudges, and talk intelligently and entertainingly.

This evening, when Agnes let him in, her deeply-lined face seemed even more ravaged than usual. Looking evasively over Alistair's left shoulder as she spoke to him, she said in a low voice, 'He's in the garden. He isn't working, he's walking up and down. I can't tell you how it gets on my nerves. Perhaps you can stop him. It does no good to keep walking, walking. What does it all matter, after all? Yes indeed, what does it matter, at least to us? So do see if you can stop him and make him sit down sensibly. You'll find him in the garden.'

She almost shut the door in Alistair's face.

Taking the path round the house to the little square of lawn behind it, he found Henry, as Agnes had said, walking slowly, heavily, from corner to corner, his gaze on the ground before him.

Hearing Alistair coming, he stood still.

'Well,' he said gloomily. 'Well.' He gave a wheezy sigh. 'What a business, eh? Horrible. Poor old Pantelaras. And the coins gone. Not

83

a word of them yet, I suppose? Don't suppose we'll ever hear of them again. Damn' shame. Can't say either how sorry I am to have let you and Rose in for all the mess. Miserable thing to happen on your holiday. How was it apart from that? Have a good time?'

'Oh yes,' Alistair said. 'Yes, fine.'

'Good. Very glad to hear it. Worried about you, naturally. How was the food?'

'Excellent.'

'Good. You're very brown. Must have had plenty of sunshine.'

'Yes.'

'Splendid. So did we, matter of fact. Too much, to judge by what they tell you. The farmers, you know. And they say the water situation's very serious up in Manchester.' He mopped his high bald forehead with his coat-sleeve. 'Well,' he said helplessly.

'I expect you want to hear how it all happened, don't you?' Alistair said.

'Well, if you don't mind . . . Interested, naturally, though it can't make any difference now. Can't quite believe in it all somehow, but perhaps when you've told me. . . . All a lot of trouble for you though, and you've had enough already.' He turned towards the house. 'Come indoors. Agnes'll make us some coffee.'

Wishing that he would stay in the garden,

84

Alistair followed him. But it was typical of the Wallbanks and the lack of comfort in which they chose to live, that they possessed no garden chairs.

They went into the living-room and sat down uneasily on the hard chairs covered in imitation leather, while Agnes, whispered to by Henry through the kitchen door, started to make some coffee.

Alistair, remembering that he had not yet asked this question, said, 'How's Agnes?'

'Not so bad,' Henry said. 'Bit nervy, of course, but her back's much better. Lucky, because I haven't been too well myself. Had to take a day or two in bed last week, and can't say I really feel myself yet. But that's partly this shocking business. Can't stop thinking about it. Poor old Pantelaras, most people didn't care for him, but he and I got along all right. Interested in the same things, of course—that always helps. You saw him, did you? Dead, I mean.'

Alistair murmured something sympathetic about Henry's health, then began to tell him of the events in Monte Carlo.

But he had said only a few words when Agnes's voice came shrilly from the kitchen, 'Wait, wait, I want to hear it all!'

Henry gave a resigned shrug of his shoulders and they waited.

Presently Agnes came in with the coffee, poured it out, sat down and took up some knitting. She always knitted with ferocity, her teeth clenched and her forehead in tight wrinkles. This evening, while Alistair spoke, she never glanced at him, but held her gaze fast on her flickering hands, while Henry, as he so often did when Agnes was present, sat watching her instead of his visitor. He watched her with a dim, bewildered stare, as if he could not understand how she had happened to him, and also as if he dared not think what else might happen if he let her out of his sight for a moment.

It made them, Alistair thought, a remarkably difficult couple to talk to. Telling them of the first unsuccessful visit to Nikolo Pantelaras, then of the second visit, of the ringing of the door-bell and the appearance of the girl, a story which by now he tended to tell in a set formula of words, he found himself wondering if he was holding their attention. Henry from time to time said, 'Well.' He said it with what sounded to Alistair like growing indifference, and it seemed plain that he was not much affected by the death of the old collector, was not interested in who had committed the murder, and, once he had heard that there was no immediate hope of recovering the coins, felt that he knew the worst and need not try to summon up any great interest in further details.

Agnes said nothing at all until near the end of the story, when she remarked suddenly, in a very controversial tone, 'The logical suspect is, of course, the wife. That's what they'll come round to. They'll blame the wife. They always do.'

'My dear, they've arrested the son-in-law,' Henry said.

She shook her head, keeping a fierce watch on her knitting. 'He was on the spot, it was easy. But they'll think again and let him go— you'll see. Then they'll look around for someone else. The wife, of course. Where was the wife supposed to be when it happened?'

'I've an idea she's somewhere in England,' Alistair said. 'She was English herself, and after the divorce she married again. Come to think of it, I don't remember anyone mentioning the nationality of her second husband, but for some reason I took for granted that he was English, and that she's living in England.'

'A-ah,' Agnes said with satisfaction. 'Then they'll be coming after her to England. You can be sure we haven't heard the last of it.'

Uneasily Henry glanced from his wife to Alistair.

'I suppose there's no question it *was* the son-in-law?' he said. 'Mean to say, they do seem to have acted rather fast.'

'They've a lot of evidence,' Alistair said, 'and so far as I know, there's only one fact that doesn't quite fit in. It's not much of a fact, however, and they've explained it away to their own satisfaction. It's about the coins. The point is, why should the coins ever have been taken out of the bank that day? Your letter to Pantelaras was perfectly clear. If he could read English at all, he must have understood that there was nothing to be gained by showing the collection to me. So why did he bring it home?'

Henry brought the tips of his fingers together. His gaze went up to the ceiling. After a moment he said, 'Disturbing little question.'

'Rose and I have discussed it a good deal,' Alistair said, 'and we've got a sort of theory about it. It's that Pantelaras didn't in fact bring the collection home to show me. He brought it home to show to someone else who was expected before me. But I was supposed to arrive before the other man left. He was supposed to see me and take me for the Purslem's representative, hot on the trail of the coins. That it was only me, instead of you, may have annoyed Pantelaras rather, but it wouldn't have upset the plan fundamentally. There I was, a possible buyer, to help him screw a higher price out of his other customer.' Alistair smiled. 'What's so nice about this theory, if you don't mind my saying so, is that it explains why Pantelaras offered you the collection at that suspiciously low figure. He knew you'd have to do something about it, you'd have to look into it—as you did.'

Agnes's needles stopped clicking. She raised her head and stared at Alistair.

'What a clever idea,' she said. 'What a very clever idea. I do believe he's right, don't you, Henry?'

'But what about the son-in-law?' Henry asked in a confused tone.

'Well, that's the difficulty,' Alistair admitted, getting up to leave. 'If I'm right, the son-in-law has probably been quite unjustly accused.'

'Dear me,' Henry said. 'Dear me.'

'On the other hand,' Alistair said, 'even if I'm right, he might still have been the murderer. He might have known of the plan, known that the collection would be in the house that day, and got in and done the murder before this other man, this other buyer I've imagined, arrived on the scene.'

'Yes,' Henry said. 'Yes. I see what you mean. D'you know, I shouldn't wonder if you're right. And so Pantelaras never meant to let us have the collection at all—that's the explanation, eh? He was setting a little trap for someone and we were just—well, the cheese. Dear me. Wouldn't have thought it of him. Thought perhaps he felt a certain gratitude to people here. Treated him pretty decently and all.'

Agnes began to laugh. Her laughter, as always, was a disturbing sound. Too much of her that had nothing to do with mirth or gaiety seemed to struggle through the high, whooping notes into the open.

Wiping her eyes, she said after a moment, 'Goodness me, that's one of the funniest things I've ever heard.'

'Funny?' Henry said. 'Oh—' As if he had just seen the point. 'That I was taken in like that?'

Alistair felt one of his impulses of acute sympathy for Henry.

'I'm probably all wrong,' he said. 'I said, it was just a theory. Actually there's no evidence whatever to support it—evidence, I mean, like fingerprints, or a strange man having been seen going into the house. The truth is, probably, that Pantelaras just liked to show off his collection, even to an ignoramus like me.'

Henry looked pleased with the suggestion.

90

'Shouldn't be surprised. Simplest explanations generally the best, eh? Yes, I should think that's the simple truth.'

'I never believe in simple explanations,' Agnes said. 'Life is very, very complicated. In fact, I don't know of anything more complicated than life.'

She said it seriously, but Alistair had a feeling that she was just about to go off again into another of her terrible fits of laughter. Rather hurriedly, he said good night to her and Henry, and left.

He strolled slowly homeward by the path across the park. A golden sunset behind the old manor house threw it into sharp relief against the sky, sending the shadow of the house a-sprawl over the smooth grass slope before it.

It was not one of the most beautiful houses in England. It had been added to too many times to be anything but a shapeless pile of buildings. Of the original house, splendid but primitive, built in the thirteenth century by a rich London merchant, only some vaults and the great hall remained. Of the Tudor additions, a whole wing still stood, handsome in itself, but dreadfully embellished by Victorian towers and battlements. A Georgian façade, serene and civilised, disclaimed relationship with all the barbarism that had come

91

before and after it.

Pausing in his walk to look at the house, Alistair realised that while he loved it for all that it meant in terms of human experience, he found it the hardest thing in the world to imagine how people had actually managed to live in it. He could imagine how people lived in caves, in mud-huts, in igloos and pent-houses, but how they had managed to spread their private lives over the acreage of rooms and corridors defeated him.

How had they known where to find one another? Might not years sometimes have passed without certain members of the house-hold ever coming face to face with one an-other? And that book and pair of spectacles, say, hurriedly put down by some long-ago Purslem, called to attend to some crisis of childbirth or death in some remote part of the building, how had he ever been able to remember in which of the three hundred rooms he had left them?

Well, perhaps three hundred was an exag-geration. Perhaps there weren't even two hundred rooms, or one hundred, though after the first seventy-five or so, what did it matter? And if that imaginary Purslem had never found his spectacles again, still they had probably remained in the house ever after, and Henry Wallbank would be able to tell you exactly where they were, in which glass case, and on which page listed in the catalogue; Henry, who spent his days in control of all that splendour, seeming as mighty as any of those men whose effigies in stone and in marble filled the chapel of the Purslems in the village church.

Yet every evening he had to leave it all behind him for the dreary little house in the grove of trees and poor Agnes. Poor Henry and poor Agnes, from whom one escaped with such relief.

Alistair walked on again.

He had some vague idea of dropping in on Paul Eckleston when he passed the lodge. He had decided to keep a firm hand on the throat of his private demon and Paul himself, since Alistair liked him and enjoyed his company, or at least had done so until very recently, seemed in a way his best ally. The thought of Paul's letter, it was true, the letter that Rose, with flaming cheeks, had left lying on the table between herself and Alistair, and which he had been quite unable to pick up, still troubled him whenever he let himself brood on it. Indeed, it was to that letter that the demon owed his continued existence. But it was not too difficult for Alistair to persuade himself that the letter would not be weighing on his mind if only he had had the sense to read it. Arriving at the lodge, he pushed open the gate and went up to the door. As it often was, it was wide open, but still, after knocking and calling out once or twice, Alistair recognised that there was no one at home.

As he walked on, the demon writhed free and reminded him with an unpleasant sneer that Paul had probably seen him pass on his way to the Wallbanks, and was by now almost certainly to be found sitting in the garden, under the cherry tree, with Rose.

There, in fact, Alistair found them. He saw them from the gate, as he had seen them a few weeks before, when he had brought Henry home with him from the committee meeting at the Maybush, and on many other evenings too.

Suddenly it seemed to Alistair that he had seen them sitting there like that, in the faint dusk of the long, lovely evenings, over and over again throughout this strange summer. The picture of it was printed so clearly on his mind that it seemed certain that he must have seen it more than a hundred times, a picture curiously flat in tone, without depth or perspective, in which, because of the fading light and the deep shadow under the tree, it was always impossible to read what was on the two faces as they looked towards him.

But this evening there was some change in

the picture. He knew it at once as he walked across the grass towards the tree. There was something in the atmosphere that had not been there before. There was some distortion about the two figures. Something was wrong.

When he reached them, nodding a restrained greeting to Paul and dropping into a chair, he saw that a part of what was distorted and wrong was the tension and the angularity in Rose, as she leant back in a pose which should have looked relaxed, yet which, in fact, looked as if she had been arrested in the middle of some impetuous movement. Her eyes, raised to Alistair's, looked abnormally bright and hard.

Leaning forward to pour him out a drink, she said jerkily, 'I've just been telling Paul the whole horrible story. He says he hadn't heard anything about it.'

Paul also seemed to speak with awkwardness. 'I don't seem to have seen anything of Henry since you went away. He didn't rush around with the news. I believe he's been ill. Agnes couldn't manage alone, so she borrowed my charwoman.'

'How was Agnes to-night?' Rose asked Alistair.

'Difficult,' he answered, taking the drink, but unable to go on looking directly at either Rose or Paul. Leaning back, he gazed up into the dark, still shadows under the leaves. 'Incredible summer,' he remarked. 'The water situation in—'

'Don't say it!' Paul said. He was in flannels and one of his check shirts, open at the neck, and was very brown. 'It's the morbid, puritanical streak in us all. We can't bring ourselves to enjoy anything without thinking about what we'll have to pay for it.'

Alistair closed his eyes. He would not, he told himself, read anything into that but a mild joke about the weather.

Yet Paul, he thought, was someone who certainly had a puritan streak in him. If ever a man was afraid of his own feelings, he was. You could see it in the lined, taut face, that sometimes seemed to be wearing those positive, strongly marked eyebrows and the horn-rimmed spectacles like a disguise. You could hear it in the quiet, carefully controlled voice, a voice which was hardly ever allowed to hesitate, to shake, to give him away. And a puritan sometimes, by a refinement of self-denial, likes to outrage his own puritanism, and then, lacking all balance and judgment, becomes dangerous.

Alistair opened his eyes again.

'Does Paul know about Irene?' he asked Rose.

'I don't know,' Rose said. 'Do you, Paul?'

'That she's coming here to open the fête on Saturday?' All the little wrinkles on Paul's face deepened and gave him, with his high, bald forehead, a wizened old-man look as he smiled lop-sidedly. 'I could hardly help knowing it, since it's been advertised in big red letters on all the posters—and there's one stuck on to one of the lodge gates where I couldn't have missed it even if I hadn't gone out. Well, I wish you luck with her. She'll probably do the job very well.'

'She's going to spend the week-end with us,' Rose said.

'Which is a polite warning to me to stay away?'

She did not answer.

He went on, 'Of course, I'm a big boy now, I know how to behave myself. But you know Irene.'

'Perhaps all this success she's had recently will have made her grow up a little too,' Alistair suggested.

'Does success do that to people?' Paul asked with elaborate innocence.

'It does sometimes, doesn't it, if you find you're getting as much attention as you want?'

'That's something Irene will never get,' Paul said.

'Well, she's arriving on Friday afternoon,

and we'll probably ask some people in for drinks to meet her,' Rose said.

'And I'm invited?'

She hesitated, then said, 'If you want to come. But if you don't, you needn't invent an excuse.'

'That's very satisfactory. I'll probably come, unless . . .' Paul looked at Alistair, who was again gazing up into the shadows over his head. 'Unless, on second thoughts, I think it may spoil your party. It could be amusing for me, but not particularly agreeable for you.'

'If she makes a scene, our guests will feel they're getting real value,' Alistair said.

'Well, if you put it like that . . . But perhaps those scenes are more my fault than I like to think,' Paul said. 'Perhaps I egg her on. I'll be very careful not to, if I come. You know, I loved that girl once. I thought she had all the beauty and sweetness and talent in the world. And part of our trouble, I dare say, is that I can't forgive her for having made me recognise that she's unreliable, dishonest, meanly ambitious and vulgar. Yet not excessively. Not so very much more than most people. And in most people I forgive it quite easily. It's just that she happens to be Irene . . . Well, good night.'

He stood up.

Alistair said that there was no reason why he should leave so early, but Paul replied that he supposed that they were tired after their journey, their murder and all. In passing Rose, he let his hand rest for an instant on her shoulder, then he said, 'Good night, Alistair.'

Alistair got up and walked with him to the gate. They chatted there for a moment about the certainty that the weather would break before the week-end, then Paul walked away into the dusk.

Alistair walked back to his chair under the tree. He walked quickly, his hands thrust into his pockets and clenched there. He had suddenly made up his mind to tell Rose straight out that he knew Paul was in love with her and to ask her what she intended to do about it.

That was as far as he meant to go. He had not yet really asked himself squarely what Rose's feelings for Paul might be, so how could he ask her about them?

But all three chairs under the tree were empty. Rose had gone into the house.

Dizzy with thankfulness, Alistair gulped down his drink and poured out another.

CHAPTER SEVEN

The weather did not break. Contrary to all forecasts, one day of sunshine followed another. Thunder was foretold and in some parts of the country actually occurred. London had a violent storm and only ten miles on the far side of the nearby town of Floxsted, a black cloud emptied itself suddenly on to the thirsty fields. But while this was happening, the sky over Rollway stayed as blue as ever. In the field where the fête and flower show were to be held on Saturday, the grass was as patchy and brown as if it had already been trampled by the hoped-for crowds.

Alistair was caught in the storm in London. He had gone up in the middle of the week, not because there was any serious necessity for him to do so at the beginning of August, but rather because he suffered from the need, felt by most academic people, to reassure themselves continuously that the institutions by which they are employed are still standing where they had left them. Or so Rose stated, claiming that at the moment Alistair's services were needed far less by his department than they were in the garden,

100

which, in spite of the drought, had had time, during their holiday, to sprout a shocking collection of weeds.

Returning by train in the evening, Alistair was inclined to think that she had been right. With almost everyone on holiday, the building had been all but empty, and if any problems had arisen during his absence, they had been coped with by his very competent secretary. Then just as he had been leaving, he had been cornered by a visiting professor from Chile, and had been held helpless in the iron grip of his conversation until all hope of catching his usual train had been lost.

Finally, when he had telephoned Rose to tell her of this and to warn her that he would be late for dinner, she had said something that had bewildered and worried him very much.

'Alistair, what does a picture of an owl mean—an owl inside a circle?'

'What—?' he had begun, then had asked her to repeat what she had said.

But she had not done so.

'It's just a letter we've had, an odd sort of letter,' she said. 'Never mind about it now. You can see it when you get home.'

'Who's it from?' he had asked.

'I don't know.'

'What d'you mean, you don't know?'

'Never mind. You'll see it this evening. But you don't know what it means—an owl inside a circle?'

'Do you mean it's a badge, or a trademark, or something?'

'I don't know. Well, don't be too late if you can help it.'

There had been an urgency in that last sentence which would not have been there if all that had been on her mind had been the length of time that the dinner would keep without spoiling.

When he reached home, she came to meet him at the door, holding a piece of paper out to him. He looked at it in surprise. It was not a letter at all. It was simply a plain sheet of cheap paper with a circle, about half an inch in diameter, drawn in the middle of it in pencil, and inside the circle the picture of an owl. There was no writing of any kind on the paper.

'Where's the envelope?' Alistair asked.

Rose picked up an envelope that had been lying on the hall table. It also was of cheap white paper, and all it had on it were the words, 'Prof. and Mrs. Dirke,' also in pencil and in scrawled capital letters.

'So it didn't come by post,' he said.

'No, some child pushed it in at the letter-box just a short time before you rang up.'

'Oh, a child,' he said. 'Then it's just a trick. One of the gang from South Rollway.'

'A child didn't draw that,' Rose said.

He looked at the paper more carefully. His first impression had been that the drawing was a distinctly childish one. The circle was uneven and the owl had a lopsided look and great pop-eyes. But now, as he studied it, he realised that the drawing was firm and skilful and that its primitiveness was, without question, intentional. Similarly, the letters on the envelope were not the carefully drawn block letters of a child, but had been dashed off roughly by a competent hand. It was puzzling. But also its effect on Rose was puzzling. She was too dismayed, too worried.

'I don't understand it at all,' he said. 'Did you see what child brought it?'

'No, I just heard a knock at the door and feet running away and I almost didn't bother to go to the door at all, because I thought it was only some of the usual silliness,' she said. 'Then, after all, I did go and I found this. I thought at first it was the bill for the newspapers. Mr. Green's little boy does sometimes bring the bills round for him just about that time. But by the time I'd realised it wasn't a bill and had rushed out into the road, I could only see a group of children a long way off already. And even close-to, that

103

mob all look so alike to me that I'm never sure which is which.'

'It must be some child's doing,' Alistair said, against his own conviction. 'A sort of Black Spot, or something like that. There's no imaginable sense in it otherwise.'

'Whatever it is, I don't like it,' Rose said.

'That's because it's anonymous. I should think there's always something rather frightening about an anonymous letter, even one that doesn't seem to mean anything in particular. But there's no point in worrying about it.'

'No.' She turned towards the kitchen. 'Let's eat. It's all ready.'

They ate, as they usually did, in the kitchen. An absent look in Rose's eyes showed that she had not stopped trying to think of possible explanations of the owl in the circle, while Alistair, beginning to be haunted by a feeling that somewhere, at some time, he had heard of, or seen, some object that the drawing resembled, kept trying to jerk his memory into throwing up to the surface whatever it was that was causing the feeling.

They were drinking coffee when Rose, lifting her brooding face, said suddenly, 'You know what I think will happen. There'll be another letter. It'll be just the same, only there'll be some words under the owl. And then there'll be another, with more words still. And they won't be nice words.'

'I know what you mean,' Alistair said.

'Only *why* should anyone do such a thing to us?' she demanded, her voice unsteady. 'Why's everything going wrong all of a sudden?'

'Everything hasn't gone wrong,' he said.

'Don't you think so? You can take murder in your stride, can you? And robbery? And suspicion?' There was hysterical irony in her voice.

'Who's suspecting who?' Alistair asked sharply.

She stared at him hard for a moment, with astonishing antagonism in her eyes. Then she gave a sigh.

'I wish I could be certain,' she said.

'Are we still talking about the murder?' he asked.

'I don't know. Are we?'

'If we aren't, I don't know . . .' He stopped himself, because of what he might say next, and as if this jerk to his thoughts liberated the memory he had been seeking, he heard himself exclaim, 'The owl—the owl of Athens!'

'Now I really don't know what you're talking about,' Rose said wearily.

'It's a coin,' he said. 'It had a head of

Athene on one side and an owl on the other. I forget its real name, but it was generally called an owl, somewhere around four or five hundred years B.C.'

'I thought you didn't know anything about coins,' Rose said.

'I don't. It's just a scrap of history that got stuck in my head—probably because I liked to think of those Greeks having their owls, as we've got our bobs and tanners.'

She gave a slight smile. 'Somehow an awful lot of education got poured into you, one time and another, and I must say, it does seem to come in useful—apart, I mean, from the fact that we live on it. But, Alistair—' The smile had disappeared. 'If you're right, if that drawing's a drawing of a coin, then it *is* connected with that business in Monte Carlo. I felt it was from the start, though I couldn't make sense of it.'

'Of course it must be,' he said.

'Yet sent to us by someone in Rollway!'

He raised a hand to stop her before she could plunge any farther. 'Let's try to think this out,' he said. 'First of all, who knows enough about the whole affair to have sent it to us?'

'Henry,' she said.

'Yes, and Agnes.'

'They don't believe what you told them

about the murder,' she went on. 'Henry thinks you know something about the coins—perhaps even that you've got them yourself. And that letter's his way of telling you so, and probably of starting to blackmail you.'

Alistair laughed wildly. 'For God's sake, Rose, think what you're saying!'

'That's what I'm doing.'

'But that would mean he'd gone quite insane.'

'Well? I can think of more unlikely things to happen.'

'No, it's ridiculous—though at a pinch I can see Agnes doing it,' he said.

'Doesn't it have to be one or the other? I don't think they've spread the news around the village. Unless, of course, you think Paul might have done it!'

Her cheeks had flamed as she flung the words at him, and it struck Alistair that she had spoken Paul's name as if it hurt her to say it.

'Of course not—he isn't mad either,' he muttered, got up and left the kitchen.

He went to the sitting-room and picked up the telephone. The exchange, which seldom hurried itself, had not yet replied when Rose appeared at the door.

'Whom are you ringing up?' she asked.

'Henry,' he said. 'I want to ask him if I'm right about that being a picture of an Athenian owl. I've never actually seen one.'

She came towards him. 'Please don't,' she said.

'Why not?'

'I'm not sure why not. I just know I don't want to tell anyone else about it yet.'

He put the telephone down. She moved suddenly closer to him. He put his hands on her arms.

'What is it, Rose?' he asked. 'Why does this thing frighten you so?'

'I don't know,' she said.

'It does, doesn't it?'

'Yes, I think it does. As you said, its being anonymous, sent by someone we know, I suppose to threaten or mock at us.'

'Perhaps it wasn't—sent by someone we know, I mean.'

'It must have been.'

'Perhaps not. But there's something more than that to it, isn't there? You've got some idea about it.'

'No,' she said.

'Rose, please—'

'No!' she said violently, and turned away from him.

Alistair went rigid, then swore quietly, walked straight out of the house and went to

108

have a drink by himself at the Maybush.

Half-way there he thought of all the people to whom he would have to talk about the weather and cricket if he went on, and, changing his mind, he went for a solitary walk through the lanes round the village.

The knowledge that Rose had some horror, real or imaginary, on her mind, which she would not confide to him, produced an unfamiliar state in him, which in some way went deeper and caused a more positive hurt than his moods of jealousy. It was not that he believed for a moment that normally she told him all her thoughts. Like himself, naturally, she had her private problems which, as much for his sake as for her own, she preferred to tackle alone, and which, he assumed, it was quite right that she should tackle alone. But still, she did not usually betray the existence of the problem quite so clearly, or underline so plainly the fact that she did not believe in his ability, or perhaps even his willingness, to help her. And what reason had she to do it now? Over this whole matter of Paul, wasn't he showing a reasonable amount of patience and understanding? Or if not, what? Yes, by God, what?

The real trouble had begun, he thought, when that letter of Paul's had reached her in Monte Carlo. Before that there had been nothing serious the matter, and what little strain there had been had been in himself rather than in Rose. But from the time that she had read that letter, she had again and again slipped into the sort of mood that she had been in this evening, resentful of him, unable to speak Paul's name without painful self-consciousness, and frightened of something. And that was what was so difficult to bear, that incomprehensible fear.

Alistair was no better than most people at imagining what the behaviour of others might be when he was not there to observe it. For the hour or so that he kept on walking, he saw Rose as sitting brooding in the room where he had left her, the expression on her face the same, frightened and evasive, as when he had seen her last.

In fact, on reaching home, he found her going about the twilit garden with a watering-can, tending a few of the most wilting plants.

She smiled when she saw him and said, 'I know this is strictly illegal, but I can't bear to see them die.'

'Yes, it's difficult,' he agreed, standing watching her as she stooped over a clump of astilbes, the leaves of which were brown and curling at the edges.

'I hope nobody's seen me,' she said. 'I started using just the washing-up water, then couldn't resist going on a bit.'

'They're probably all doing the same.'

'I expect so. You know, I don't think we'll have any wallflowers next spring unless we buy some plants. The seeds I put in have hardly grown at all.'

'Let's buy some, then. Which reminds me, did I tell you there's a rumour abroad that Mr. Tolliver's been buying onions to enter at the show?'

'No, you didn't tell me, but I heard it on the bush telegraph.'

They went on talking about the garden and about their neighbours, as they so often and contentedly did, and it was almost as if there had never been any anonymous letter pushed in at the letter-box, no murder, no distress or distrust.

For the next few days they went on and on talking about the garden and their neighbours, and at least it was better than silence.

The rumour about Mr. Tolliver's onions, Alistair discovered, was all round the village by now. Nevertheless, on Friday afternoon, Mr. Tolliver appeared serenely in the field where the fête was to be held, to help prepare it for the show. Most of the members of the Produce Association committee came too for short periods of frenzied work, and even more frenzied argument about the arrangements. The marquees, as usually happened, had been put up in the wrong places and it seemed doubtful whether the cable from the doctor's electric hedge-clipper, always loaned for this purpose, would reach from the plug in the chairman's kitchen to the urn in the tea-tent. The number of stakes loaned by a local farmer to form the ladies' and the gentlemen's bowling-alleys was quite insufficient. The bowls themselves could not be found. The firm that was to deliver the ice-cream and minerals denied having received any order.

In fact, it was an afternoon of great anxiety and great exertion, towards the end of which Paul Eckleston, who had been one of the helpers, muttered to Alistair, 'I've had about all I can take of this for the time being. What about coming home with me for a drink?'

Alistair looked at his watch. 'I'm not sure that I oughtn't to go straight home,' he said. 'Rose went to meet Irene in Floxsted. They'll be back by now and there'll be a few people arriving soon for sherry.'

'Including me,' Paul said. 'But I think I need a quiet drink on my own before I face it.' He wiped the sweat from his forehead. 'We've done enough here. Let's go.' There was a faint insistence in his tone, as if the suggestion were not really as casual as he tried to make it sound.

Alistair shrugged his shoulders and went to fetch his jacket.

They did not speak much on their way to the lodge, and when they did, it was only of the mysterious complications inherent in all democratic action, and particularly in the organisation of the Rollway village flower show and fête.

'Ramshackle business—only somehow it always turns out all right,' Paul said.

'Weather permitting,' Alistair said automatically.

'Well, there's no form of efficiency been invented yet for coping with that. Now, about Irene . . .' The level, controlled voice faltered.

Alistair waited for it to go on.

'Do many people hereabouts know we were once married, d'you think?' Paul asked after a moment.

'From the fact that I haven't heard it talked about, I should think not,' Alistair said.

'Remarkable.' Paul now sounded tired and nervous. 'I suppose if I changed my mind, if I didn't turn up this evening, you wouldn't worry.'

'Of course not,' Alistair said.

'The fact is—well—oh, I expect I'll come. But I rather wish now I hadn't said the things about Irene that I did the other evening. They've been on my mind. And they were only half true. She isn't bad. She's got her virtues, or even if she hasn't, that's no business of mine. Thank God.' He laughed queerly. 'Incidentally, I've changed my mind about something else. I've decided after all to take a holiday abroad.'

So this, Alistair thought, was the real reason why Paul had asked him to walk home with him. Paul wanted him to know that he was going away, was leaving the field clear. But for whose sake was he supposed to be doing this—for his own, for Alistair's, for Rose's? And did he expect Alistair to thank him for it?

As if the information meant nothing to him, Alistair said, 'Where are you thinking of going?'

'Sweden, I think. I'm not sure yet. I only know I want to get away for a while and I'm tired of the everlasting South.'

'That's because of this extraordinary summer.'

'This damnable summer!'

It was said so quietly that Paul might not have intended it to be heard.

As if he had not in fact heard it and as they turned in at the lodge gates, Alistair remarked, 'You never seem to lock your house up much.' For as usual the little house, just inside the gates, had most of its windows and its front door open.

Paul stood still for a moment. 'No, but I don't think I left the door actually open this time, even if I didn't lock it,' he said, and went forward quickly.

As he did so, Henry Wallbank appeared in the doorway.

Henry looked as unreasonably surprised to see Paul as Paul might have been to see him. But there was more than mere surprise on Henry's face. Though the network of little red veins that covered it prevented it from turning pale, it gave a curious impression of pallor. The mouth and the pouches under the eyes looked flabbier than usual. The eyes were vague with shock.

'Paul,' he said, as if he were not sure of it.

'Looking for me?' Paul said.

'Yes,' Henry said. 'I came to see you, to tell you . . . Well, never mind. Came, gave a knock at the door, it opened—and then, God help me, I saw *that*!'

He spun on his heel and pointed into the room.

In spite of the warmth of the evening, Alistair felt a prickling sense of cold in his body. There was a haunting feeling of familiarity in the situation, a feeling that it had all hap-

115

pened just like this before, and that therefore what was yet to come was inevitably disaster.

The iron lodge gates, the door that had opened at a touch, these belonged in some story that he had already heard and of which he knew the ending.

He followed Paul into the room. Then he stood still, shocked, though not as his nerves had expected to be shocked. Looking at the figure before him, the figure of a man, thin, grey and fragile, with a great grey face that hung like a mask, fantastically topped by pie-bald black and white hair, between his narrow shoulders, Alistair found himself laughing helplessly.

For this figure, at which they were all staring, as if it were the ghost of a murdered man, was of terra-cotta and was only six inches tall.

CHAPTER EIGHT

It stood on the top of an open walnut bureau, facing them, between a tortoiseshell tea-caddy and a vase of beautifully etched glass that held a few roses.

The room was a small one, but everything in it had been chosen with care, and if it had been a little less untidy, the effect would have been of comfort and charm, and as unlike that of the Wallbanks' cheerless home as was possible. Yet the two little houses had been built in much the same style, a stolid red brick Victorian, with a faint craziness of Gothic about it.

Except for the figure on the mantelpiece, there was none of Paul's work to be seen, and that that figure should be there at once struck Alistair as singular. Paul had a peculiar dread of showing off his work to his friends. Sometimes, on an impulse, he might take someone out to the studio in the garden and enter on a long, excited explanation of techniques, but usually he was evasive, to the point of secretiveness, about what he did there.

'Well?' he said fiercely to Henry, and, to judge by the tightening of his features, was preparing himself to meet unfavourable criticism.

'Well!' Henry echoed. 'You know—*don't* you know?—what happened to him!'

'Yes, I know,' Paul said defensively.

'Damn' thing's genius!' Henry exclaimed. 'Absolute genius. But, good God—!' He was breathing heavily. Raising a hand, he pointed with a thick, slightly shaking finger at the little terra-cotta figure of Nikolo Pantelaras. 'Man was murdered and you go and put an image of him . . .' He swallowed. He could be seen trying to calm his nerves. 'Thought you only did this sort of thing from the life,' he muttered.

'I don't do much of this sort of thing at all,' Paul said.

'But I remember your saying—'

'I know, I know—that evening in the Dirkes' garden,' Paul said. 'Well, the few times I've tried these things, it's been from the life. But that evening I started thinking about the old man. . . .' He stopped, looking annoyed with himself for having started to enter on an explanation of his actions. 'What did you want me for, anyway?'

Henry, as if hypnotised, was still staring at the figure.

'Genius,' he repeated. 'Even if it's horrible.'

'It isn't the one or the other,' Paul said

impatiently. 'Genius or horrible.'

'Don't mean horrible,' Henry said. 'Not the thing itself. But sitting there, looking at it . . . Well, that's your business, of course. Sorry to get so worked up. Couldn't do it myself at the moment for all the tea in China. Suppose I'll get over it, but just at the moment, when the old man's just been knocked off and there's that young fellow in gaol over there, going to be guillotined, I suppose, and the collection gone God knows where. . . . Such beautiful things, you know. Exquisite pieces. Can't stop myself thinking about it—particularly as I can't stop Agnes talking about it. Got her so excited, you'd think she was half enjoying it all. Well, well. Oh yes, you asked me why I wanted you. That wasn't important. Just wanted you to tell the committee there's a rumour around that Tolliver's going to enter some onions for the show that he bought over at the show at Nether Lipton. Story goes he hasn't got any onions in his garden this year. Been too busy myself to get over and tell anyone.'

Tearing his gaze away from the little figure on the mantelpiece, Henry gave Paul a glassy-eyed stare and turned to the door.

'Just a minute, Henry,' Alistair said. 'There was something I wanted to ask you. Am I right that certain Greek coins had an

119

owl on them?'

'Yes,' Henry said. 'Why?'

'Just general interest,' Alistair said.

'Yes, the owl of Athens. Badge of the city. Owl on one side, head of Athene on the other. Used for centuries. Well, see you later.'

Henry plunged out into the garden.

Paul strolled across the little room to the bureau, which was an untidy litter of papers. Picking up the terra-cotta figure, he looked for a moment as if he were considering hurling it down on the hearth. Then he gave a rather sheepish smile at Alistair, put the figure into an empty pigeon-hole in the bureau, closed the flap and sketched a movement of washing his hands of the matter.

'Why the "general interest" in owls?' he asked.

'Well, coins are in the air, aren't they?'

Paul gave the smile that made his face look wizened. 'You don't lie very well. But your business, of course, as Henry would probably say.' He opened the tortoiseshell tea-caddy, which he used as a cigarette-box, and took a cigarette out of it. 'Did it shock you too, seeing that thing here? You actually saw the man dead, after all.'

'Yes, in a way it did,' Alistair said.

'You haven't said what you think of it.'

'It's very good.'

'Not genius?'

Alistair smiled.

Paul gave a laugh, lighting his cigarette. 'Henry's got very interested in my genius recently. He suggested I might have a show of some of my stuff in one of the Purslem galleries. Nice of him. So I've been working harder than usual. This is some of the results. But could you ever manage to get as worked up as Henry is about losing a lot of coins that were never going to belong to you anyway— to yourself personally, I mean, but only to the Purslem Collection?'

'If I were Henry, yes, I'd think of the Purslem as my home, rather than the place I'd got to go back to in the evenings,' Alistair said.

Paul shook his head. 'It wouldn't be the same thing. Or at least, I can't imagine it. That may be my limitation. I expect you'll hear a lot about my limitations this evening from Irene.'

'I gather you really don't want to meet her,' Alistair said.

Paul seemed not to hear him. He puffed some smoke out, looking thoughtfully towards the bureau in which he had shut the figure away. 'She always said I was bad at sharing my pleasures with others,' he said. 'She always said I ought to live alone. And she may have been right, particularly as what she probably really meant was that my income was only large enough for me to live alone. That's true, at any rate.'

Alistair's mind did a violent see-saw between anger and bewilderment. Had Paul brought him here to tell him that he did not intend to make love to his wife simply because he could not afford to support her? Was he capable of that? Or was Alistair himself becoming too dexterous at reading double meanings into all that was said to him, making a sort of Great Pyramid, with all its secret messages waiting for interpretation, out of the most innocent conversation?

Not that this conversation with Paul felt particularly innocent. There was something at the back of it, though Alistair was still not sure what it was.

Paul went on, 'It's difficult for me now even to imagine what it was like being married to her. And I can't think to this day what she saw in me. I saw her beauty and vitality, but what there was in me . . . It was wartime, of course, and I was in uniform, which may have disguised some of my normal characteristics. My timidity, I mean, and my general lack of ambition and so on. She may even have worked it out that I was rich. As a matter of fact, I thought so myself then. We all talked about rising prices, didn't we, but we'd no idea really what that could mean. I could have taken a job, I suppose, though I don't know what at—an art-master, perhaps—but somehow I doubt if that would have satisfied Irene.'

'It's odd your saying that,' Alistair said, irritated at the self-pity in Paul's voice, 'because I should have thought that of all the people I know, Irene's as nearly indifferent to money as any. I imagine she's enjoying her success, now that it's come to her, but she never seemed particularly distressed at having to be a waitress, or a shopgirl, or any of the other things she used to try her hand at when she couldn't get a job in the theatre.'

Paul gave a laugh. 'No one's indifferent to money. But you're lucky—you don't know how lucky you are, Alistair—having a sale-able talent, a mental kink, if you don't mind my putting it like that, which you enjoy using and which earns you a steady and quite decent income. Now I've a talent and be-tween ourselves I'll say it's not an altogether inconsiderable one. . . .' He gestured to-wards the bureau. 'But there's no money in it. None to speak of.'

'There may be some day.'

'When I'm dead? When my work begins to wander into antique shops and the lesser known museums? Oh, a lot of money!'

'I meant as you become better known.' Alistair went towards the door. 'Are you coming back with me or not?'

Paul ignored the question. In a soft voice he said, ' "The owl and the pussy-cat went to sea in a beautiful pea-green boat. They took some honey and plenty of money . . ." ' He broke off, springing to his feet. 'No, I don't think I'll come, if you don't mind. Then Irene won't have any excuse for spoiling your party.'

'But you'll see her to-morrow at the fête?'

'Shall I? Yes, I suppose so. Yes, of course.'

'You *are* coming to the fête? You're selling the ices and minerals, I believe,' Alistair said.

'Oh yes, I take my duties seriously,' Paul answered.

'Then we'll see you to-morrow.'

Alistair stepped out into the garden. Just as he left, he had a last glimpse of Paul's face, taking on the blankness of complete abstraction.

So one interpretation, Alistair thought, as he started for home, of what had been strange in the conversation, was that Paul's mind really had not been on anything that he had been saying, but had been intensely occupied with something that he did not intend to communicate at all.

There was a certain relief for Alistair in the fact that Paul had decided to avoid Irene that evening. Yet Irene herself, flying straight into Alistair's arms as soon as she heard him at the door, planting kisses on various parts of his face, then standing back to look at him, exclaimed in consternation, 'But where's Paul, darling? Where's my frightful, darling Paul? Rose said you were bringing him. Oh, don't tell me, don't tell me that he can't bear to see me!' And she looked as if she were going to burst into tears.

But of course you always had to remember that grain of salt when you were dealing with Irene. She could have had this scene carefully rehearsed in case Paul should not appear, and at the same time could have had another, a very different scene, ready in case he did.

However, with her bright little face starting to crumple, and a threat of moisture in her eyes, her disappointment, for the moment, seemed entirely sincere. She was a small woman, very slender, very fair and fragile-looking, though she possessed, Alistair believed, the energy of a team of cart-horses and the toughness of a tank.

Letting go of him abruptly now, she went running like an athlete, on her very high heels, back to Rose in the sitting-room.

'He hates me, Rose!' she cried. 'I told you

125

so. He's never forgiven me.'

'Well, why should he?' Rose asked. 'Your way of speaking about him doesn't overflow with forgiveness.'

'Oh, the way I *speak!*' Irene said. 'But I'd never go out of my way to avoid him—I mean, positively go out of my *way* to do it. I'd never think of doing anything so humiliating to him. I might slap his face, I might throw something at him, but I'd never, never just avoid him. Would I have come here at all if I were capable of doing such a thing?'

'Perhaps he doesn't enjoy dodging the crockery,' Rose said. She looked at Alistair. 'Isn't he coming?'

He shook his head. He was entertained, as he always had been, by the sight of Rose and Irene together, for if ever a friendship had been founded on the attraction of opposites, this one surely had, and each woman always seemed to produce in the other an exaggeration of her natural characteristics. Rose, at the moment, was looking more than normally calm and composed, Irene even more dramatically emotional than usual. Rose, in a white linen dress, which heightened the warm tones of her sun-tanned skin, seemed, beside Irene, to acquire an almost milk-maidish air of having been born and bred in the country. Irene, in black shantung fitting close as a glove to her small, beautifully shaped body, became in contrast a pure expression of urban artifice and nerves.

That the truth about them was that they had both been born in the same suburb of a Midland town, and had gone to the same school there, could not have been detected in the personality of either.

'Well, how are you, Irene?' Alistair asked. 'You're looking very beautiful.'

'I feel terrible, darling,' she answered. 'I do. I've got a suspicion I'm seriously ill. I get the most frightful shooting pain from my diaphragm right the way up to the top of my head—I almost scream when it happens— just at any odd time. It feels as if I were being sliced in two.'

'Then you must get together with Agnes,' he said. 'You'll find each other very interesting.'

'Who's Agnes?'

'You'll be meeting her presently. A woman with more ailments than anyone you've ever met.'

'The poor thing,' Irene said warmly. 'I'll be glad to meet her. Perhaps I can cheer her up. Oh, you can laugh if you want to, but I like cheering people up and I know what it is to suffer. But you always had a cynical sort of nature, darling, hadn't you? You can't be

127

simple and serious about simple and serious things.'

'Well, I hope you won't get sliced in two before to-morrow,' he said. 'If it rains, you'll be the only thing between the Produce Association and bankruptcy.'

'Darling, you can count on me whatever happens, you know that,' she said. 'I think it's terribly important never to let people down. The more they expect of you, the more you've got to give them. And they expect so much of me now, you know, now that I'm successful.' With a sudden crow of mirth, she shed her fearful gravity. 'I *am* successful— d'you realise that? D'you realise how bloody successful I am? My God, it feels wonderful!' And she thumped herself hard on just about the spot where she said the terrible shooting pain was liable to begin. 'That bastard Paul's jealous of me, that's why he won't come to see me. He's green with jealousy.'

'Well, I'd better go and get cleaned up a bit before people start arriving,' Alistair said and went out, leaving the two old friends together.

While he was upstairs, washing and changing, he could hear Irene's voice from below, running on and on in one of her monologues of intimate information about herself. She had a wonderfully clear and carrying voice,

128

without her seeming to raise it. Odd emphasised words, most of them rude names for men, reached him from time to time, and once he heard her cry out, on a note of wild curiosity, '*Murder?*'

So Rose, he supposed, had got in a few words about their holiday, but either her account of it had been remarkably succinct, or else Irene's curiosity was never satisfied, for the break in Irene's flow of talk was only momentary.

But when the few guests whom the Dirkes had invited started to arrive, Irene's personality underwent an instant and apparently effortless change. She became very quiet, looked a little uncertain about the propriety of accepting a glass of sherry, smiled shyly and gratefully at anyone who paid her any attention, and, to Alistair's amazement, actually settled down in a corner with Agnes for a long, heartening talk about symptoms.

He noticed, however, that again and again Irene's gaze strayed to the door, as if she were waiting for another guest to appear, and that as the time lengthened out without this happening, something sad and bewildered came into her eyes.

Agnes was in an uncommonly good humour and looking as nearly smart as it was possible to imagine her. The pink crepe dress which she used for all such occasions had recently been to the cleaners. She had on a little powder and lipstick. Her stockings, instead of being of wrinkled grey cotton, were of nylon. After one glass of sherry she began to laugh very gaily and a little inexplicably, as if she were allowing herself to enjoy openly some tremendous private joke, and Henry, who was looking particularly depressed, kept his eyes glued on her with even more desperation than usual.

But a second glass of sherry unsettled Agnes no farther, and the third, which she insisted on having, seemed to bring her to a state of friendly and poised sobriety. She told Alistair that she was feeling very well. She told the chairman of the Produce Association that she would certainly help at the fête next day. She told Rose that her friend was really charming and that she herself was looking lovely. Altogether it was one of Agnes's good days.

This interested Alistair, making him wonder, as he went round with the decanter and chatted to the people in the room, what made the difference between Agnes's good days and her bad ones. Did she perhaps become happier and healthier as Henry became less well and more despondent? It almost looked like it. And that might mean that if only

Henry could have a breakdown of some sort, Agnes might start to bloom like a flower in the desert. Only what would Agnes's blooming be like? The thought was perhaps just a little frightening.

Presently he found himself re-filling Irene's glass. She had separated from Agnes by then and had just been talking earnestly to the vicar about the boon of television to the sick and aged.

Leaning towards Alistair, she said to him in a half whisper, 'He really isn't coming, is he?'

'I'm afraid not, Irene,' he said, feeling sorry for her, though he wondered why she should be so set on seeing Paul.

'I didn't really believe you when you said so before,' she said. 'I thought you were making it up.'

'But why should I do that?' he asked.

'Oh, to annoy me, to tease me.' Her soft mouth had become tight-lipped and a little twisted.

'I really don't think that would particularly appeal to me,' he said.

'Wouldn't it? Don't you like giving the knife a twist? Most people do.'

'That seems a sad view to take.'

'Ah, you haven't gone through what I've gone through.' She had sat down on a sofa, drawing him down beside her. 'I've had to toughen myself, I've had to grow a skin like leather. You lead such a sheltered life, you and Rose, you simply won't know what I'm talking about.'

'I expect that's quite true,' he said. 'We've been pretty fortunate, I suppose.'

'Darling, I could cry with envy,' she said, 'except that I'd be so scared of something going wrong. Now things can go wrong as hell with me and I just take it in my stride. But you and Rose . . .' She paused, looking at him through the smoke of her cigarette. 'Something is wrong, of course. What is it? Is it Paul?'

He started and she went on at once, 'Oh, don't worry. Rose hasn't been talking. She isn't the kind who talks, even when you've talked and talked to her about yourself enough to make her forget herself once in a while. But I could tell. There was a look on her face every time I mentioned Paul.'

Alistair said nothing.

'I won't say I know what the look meant, exactly,' Irene said. 'Looks are sometimes deceptive, aren't they?'

'That, at least, is true,' he muttered.

'Oh, you're angry,' she said. 'Well, never mind. But that's the real reason Paul hasn't come, isn't it? It's something to do with

132

Rose.'

Alistair was very angry now. That Irene's shrewd little mind should pounce straight on to what he believed was the correct explanation of Paul's behaviour that day, made him seethe with fury against her and himself.

He thought of Paul's sudden desire to go to Sweden, of the way that he had changed his mind about coming to the party, of his bitter statement of his inability to share his pleasures with others, of the way that he had talked about his poverty. It all meant, it must mean, that some time during the last day or two there had been some kind of a showdown between him and Rose.

Perhaps, Alistair thought, it had happened on the day that he had gone to London and coming home, had found Rose so distraught about a ridiculous drawing of an owl. A purely ridiculous drawing, a child's trick. Would he ever have taken it seriously if he had not been infected by Rose's extraordinary tension and distress?

But at that point he tried to put a brake on his thoughts. He was confusing things. Even if most of Rose's nervous excitement that day had come from something that had happened between herself and Paul, there was still something very peculiar and unpleasant about the owl. And why, after all, should he

133

be working himself up into such a rage when the one thing that seemed certain was that Rose had sent Paul about his business? True, she had not confided in Alistair, and her secret had hammered a wedge of silence, or, if you preferred that name for it, of gardening talk, between them.

'You talk the most unmitigated nonsense,' he said to Irene.

'You aren't the first who's said so,' she agreed.

'What are you going to tell us all at this show to-morrow?'

'Oh, just what wonderful, wonderful people you all are.'

'We'll like that.'

'Of course you will. But listen, you mustn't worry about Paul. He's got great fascination, I know. All that diffidence of his brings out the maternal in women, while his independence is a sort of challenge to them. But it doesn't last. I mean, he's never married again, has he? Which he would have done if he'd got the sort of qualities that you've got. I mean, the *real* things.'

'Thanks.'

'He's too selfish, you know, too wrapped up in himself. That's all right in a young man. There's a fearsome thrill about gigantic selfishness in a young man. But in a middle-aged man it's just tiresome.'

'I'll try to remember that.'

'Oh, you don't need to. One can trample all over you. But now tell me, do you think Paul actually hates me? Do you think if it hadn't been for Rose, he would have come here this evening?' Her voice grated a little, not with a sound of anger, but rather as if she were trying to keep a tremor out of it.

He put a hand on one of hers. 'You'll see him tomorrow—if that really matters to you.'

'Oh, it doesn't *matter*,' she said quickly. 'But to be hated, you know—to be actually hated so much that a person can't bear to see one—that's too much. But he'll be at this fête of yours, will he?'

'He's selling the ices and minerals.'

As if this conjured up a picture of fantastic comedy, she gave a crow of laughter.

She had been so quiet till then that everyone in the room suddenly looked at her.

In the little silence that occurred, the front-door bell rang.

Irene was on her feet in an instant. But Rose was the nearer to the door and was out of the room before Irene had taken a couple of steps. She stood still, then quietly sat down on the sofa again and resumed her talk with Alistair. He did his best to answer her, ready to help her, if that was what she wanted, to appear to be in the midst of a normal conversation when Paul came in.

Then he heard a woman's voice from the hall and realised that the new arrival was not Paul.

A moment later two people came into the room with Rose. One was a small, plump elderly woman in a dress of purple and green flowered cotton, with several strings of lilac-coloured plastic beads round her neck. The other, walking jerkily at her side, was a small, stringy, grey-haired man.

From behind them Rose's eyes met Alistair's with a look of warning. But her voice was particularly warm and friendly as she said, '*Isn't* it nice of the Griffins to have remembered us?'

CHAPTER NINE

Mrs. Griffin was all apologies.

'If we'd had the faintest idea you were having a party,' she said, 'we'd never have walked in on you like this. And we won't stay a moment. . . . No, I mean it, we really won't stay. We're spending the night in Floxsted, at the Red Lion, on our way home by easy stages. We'd hoped perhaps you'd come out to dinner with us, that's why we dropped in. But of course we'd never have bothered you if we'd known you had friends with you.'

Alistair said that that was the best time of all to come, and Rose told the Griffins that she was perfectly delighted to see them and asked why shouldn't they stay to dinner. Mrs. Griffin said they could not possibly impose themselves on her for dinner, but if they might, they'd just stay for a drink and a chat.

Rose said that would be lovely and added that she and Alistair had missed the Griffins dreadfully during the last few days of their holiday, and had been hoping ever since that some time they might meet again.

'Of course, Floxsted *is* a little out of our

way,' Mrs. Griffin said, when she and her husband had been introduced to the other guests and had expressed their astonishment and delight at meeting Irene Byrd. 'So I suppose you're wondering why we really came. Well, I'll tell you. We got bitten by a new bug in Italy—you know we went on to Italy when we left Cap Martin? My husband got bitten by it so badly that I hardly know what to do with him. He's gone mad, absolutely mad, on sight-seeing. And so he said, when we landed at Dover, why do we have to stop this simply because we're in England again? There are all kinds of things in England I've always wanted to see, he said, but never really had the chance to develop the taste till I retired. But now we've a wonderful opportunity, he said, so let's stop at all the castles and museums and cathedrals on our way home. And that's what we've been doing. And we came here, of course, to take a look at the wonderful Purslem Collection, at least, that was part of the reason, because as soon as my husband picked it out in the guidebook, I said, but that's where those charming Dirkes live, oh yes, we must go there. And here we are.'

Mr. Griffin gave a jerky nod, smiled, sipped some sherry and said, 'Wonderful collection. Interesting old house too. Beautiful park.'

As if he had received a personal compliment, Henry Wallbank's face turned red. He shifted from foot to foot, made vague embarrassed movements with his hands, and said, 'Glad to take you round it properly myself to-morrow morning, if you're staying on. Glad to. Delighted. Hope I can have the privilege.'

'There now!' Mrs. Griffin exclaimed. 'Oh, if only we'd known! We've been wandering around it all this afternoon, Mr. Wallbank, just two ignorant tourists on our own. And if only we'd waited we could have had you to take us round? Why, I could almost cry when I think of what we've missed.'

'But you don't mean you're going straight on to-morrow!' Rose said in consternation. 'Oh, you can't do that, Mrs. Griffin. Now that you've got here, you'll have to stay at least the week-end.'

'My dear, that's sweet of you,' Mrs. Griffin said, 'considering the way we've just thrust ourselves on you. And there's nothing I'd like better, but I'm not the one who decides that sort of thing. Am I, Bill?' She appealed to her husband. 'Bill's been saying we've got to get home to-morrow.'

Rose turned to him. 'I'm sure you haven't really got to, Mr. Griffin. Just think what it's like, driving at the weekend. But if you wait till it's over, you'll have quiet roads and a nice drive.'

In Alistair's ear, Irene murmured, 'How she loves your new friends, darling, whoever they are.'

'So it seems,' he agreed.

'Perhaps she got bitten by a new bug of some sort in France,' she went on, 'because at the moment she's acting right out of character.'

And that was certainly true, though Rose was acting the part with determination. She was using all her powers of persuasion to induce the Griffins to remain in Rollway for the week-end, and she showed great satisfaction when, behind a continuing screen of apologies, they weakened and agreed to stay for at least one more day. But they would not stay to dinner and when each had drunk a glass of sherry, they insisted on leaving.

Soon afterwards, the other guests left. Rose and Alistair saw them out to their cars, then returned to Irene, who, after a bout of handshaking and of sweet and eager expressions of her delight at having met them all, had shed her gentility like a waterproof after a shower, and with a drink in her hand, a cigarette hanging from her lip and one hand clawing through her smooth, bright hair, had a familiar air of raffish vitality.

'This, believe me, is very, very suspicious!' she declared. 'I want to be told what's at the back of it all. You two go off to France, you have a murder all to yourselves there, you meet these Griffin characters, who, if you don't mind my saying so, are all very well, but not just the type one would expect to find were your bosom friends, unless you've both changed completely since I saw you last—'

'Perhaps we have,' Rose interrupted. She went to the table where the drinks were. 'I'm going to have another drink. We always need a quiet drink on our own when our visitors have gone—then I'll get us something to eat.'

'Yes, darling,' Irene said. 'But ignoring your attempt to change the subject and returning to the Griffins, they follow you here, they force themselves in on you—and it's no good pretending they wouldn't have done it if they'd known you were having a party, because there were three or four cars out there, and I don't suppose they think you own three or four cars, or run a garage. And they natter about the Purslem Collection and their passion for museums, but when your Mr. Wallbank offers to take them round it to-morrow, they're very quick to say they've seen it already. And then Rose—Rose who's already busy enough with me and a village fête on her hands, and who, in any case,

doesn't hurl herself at other people's heads—
Rose goes and pours out pressing invitations
at those people, as if she couldn't bear the
thought that they might get away from her.
Well, what *is* it all about? Come on, I want to
be told.'

'You always talk too much to be told
anything,' Rose answered, smiling. 'What
shall we have to eat? There are some chops.
Or I could make omelettes. Or I could open a
tin of tongue.'

'That, Irene, is a polite way of telling us
that we're going to have the tin of tongue,'
Alistair said. 'And while you're getting it,
Rose, I'd better get the Joy Wheel out of the
attic and make sure it's in working order. I
ought to have done it before.'

'All right, all right, you don't want to talk,'
Irene said. 'I'm not blind, I'm not deaf—
though I think my questions are perfectly
reasonable. And what the hell is a Joy
Wheel?'

'A contraption that Rose and I will operate
at the fête to-morrow afternoon,' Alistair
answered, 'to extract pennies from the young
of South Rollway, who are desperate gam-
blers, to a man. That's a flat round board,
marked out into twelve segments, and an
arrow-shaped thing, supported at the middle,
which spins. We put little packets of sweets

on each of the segments, the children put their pennies on the one they want, we spin the arrow, and there you are. Some lucky child gets threepence worth of sweets for a penny and ninepence goes into the kitty.'

'But that's just roulette, sort of,' Irene said.

'We don't call it roulette in Rollway,' Alistair said. 'We call it a Joy Wheel.'

'I call it robbery, taking their pennies off the poor kids like that,' Irene said.

'They love it.'

'But what d'you use the money for, anyway, when you've got it?' she asked.

'For next year's fête.'

'And the money you get then for the year after?'

'Of course. You've stumbled straight on to the everlasting truth about village economics. But let me add that if we should make some enormous profit, like say ten or eleven pounds, and with a celebrity like you to open the show for us we hope very much we may achieve at least that, we shall probably treat ourselves to a nice silver cup to give as a prize at next year's flower show.'

'A silver cup!' Irene said. 'I'm worth a silver cup? You know, that makes one think!' And it seemed to make her think so hard that she forgot her curiosity about the Griffins.

Uneasily until bedtime, Alistair and Rose acted as if they were not thinking about the Griffins either, but as soon as they were alone in their room, Rose said explosively, '*They* sent it!'

'The owl? Yes, it looks as if they've been in the neighbourhood for longer than they wanted us to think,' Alistair agreed. 'And if that's so I think we ought to tell the police about the letter.'

Rose sat down at the dressing-table and gazed probingly at her own reflection, as if she were trying to decide whether or not the woman whom she saw there was of a kind likely to have taken leave of her senses. After a moment she said, 'D'you know, Alistair, I think they think we're murderers and robbers.'

He had reached this conclusion himself, but because of the excitement in her voice, he said with caution, 'They may merely think we have some information about the murder.'

'In that case, what's their own connection with it? Why should they want to know anything special about it? Why should they send us that horrible letter? Because they must have sent it. Because, if they didn't, it was sent by Henry, or Agnes, or—or Paul, and we don't believe that.'

'No,' he said.

She heard the reservation in his tone and said quickly, 'I thought you were quite sure it couldn't have been Henry.'

'It just could have been Agnes, couldn't it?' he said. 'I was looking at her this evening and thinking she's really a very strange woman. Strange and perhaps—' He hesitated, hunting for the word he wanted. 'Malign.'

Rose wrinkled her forehead. 'But now the Griffins have turned up, surely . . .'

'Oh yes,' he said, 'it's almost certainly the Griffins.'

'And they think we murdered Nikolo Pantelaras and stole his collection of coins and they've come here to blackmail us!'

At that point Alistair could not help laughing. But the laughter was hollow, because that was precisely what he had been thinking himself. Such amusement as he had actually felt had come from hearing those words spoken in that pleasant bedroom, with its windows wide open on to the moonlit garden, without even curtains drawn to provide protection against the night-quiet of the world around them.

'Unless,' Rose went on, 'they did the murder, stole the coins and cleared off into Italy. That makes just as much sense. Except why should they have come here after us instead of doing all they could to keep out of our way?' She turned towards him. 'You're trying to laugh at me for having got so panicky, but really you agree with me, don't you?'

He answered slowly, 'I suppose so. But there's no need to get panicky, is there? Since, I mean, we didn't do the murder, or steal the collection.'

'No, but all the same . . .' She turned back to the mirror, picked up her hairbrush, gave her hair a few strokes, then put the brush down again. 'Do you remember when we talked it all over the night after the murder? Do you remember we agreed the queer thing was that the coins were in the house at all, since there wasn't any point in Pantelaras showing them to us, and we thought that perhaps he'd really got them out of the bank to show someone else before us?'

'And you're thinking that might have been the Griffins?'

'No,' she said, 'because that would make them the murderers, wouldn't it? Or at least it would mean that they got away with the collection before the son-in-law got in and did the murder. And then I'm sure they wouldn't have come after us, of all people. Unless they had an idea they could sell it to us or Henry. Oh no, I don't suppose that makes sense.'

146

She started brushing her hair again. 'The only question is, really, what are we going to do about it?'

'Take the letter to the police,' he said definitely.

'To Sergeant Wragg?'

'I think we might go over his head to the people in Floxsted.'

'At once?'

'Well, to-morrow.'

'Oh, I know you didn't mean at once—to-night. But you mean before we've had any chance to talk to the Griffins privately?'

'If they were behind the letter,' he said, 'talking to them won't get us anywhere.'

'Unless they're just waiting for a chance to show their hands. And they might not do it if the police have been brought into it.'

'But the police can check up on them in all sorts of ways, which we can't. And then we can wash our hands of the whole thing.'

She gave a shiver. Putting down her hairbrush, she put both her hands to her temples. It looked rather as if she were waiting for a moment of dizziness to pass. When she went on, the excitement had gone from her voice. 'Perhaps really they're just two silly people, chasing sensation. I rather wish now I hadn't persuaded them to stay.'

'Because I think we ought to go to the

police?'

She did not answer.

'They'd have stayed anyhow, you know, without the persuading,' he said. 'But what did you mean just now, Rose, when you started to talk about the person for whom Pantelaras may really have got the coins out of the bank?'

'Nothing, really,' she said wearily.

He waited a moment, watching her perplexedly. 'D'you mean you rather badly don't want me to go to the police?'

With a sigh, she said, 'No, I suppose you ought to go. But will they take any notice, d'you think? Of the letter, I mean.'

'I rather think they will. Our connection with a murder ought to give us a certain status in their eyes.'

But next morning, at the police station in Floxsted, to which he had driven after setting up the Joy Wheel in its place on the field, he found it hard to decide how seriously the men to whom he spoke and showed the drawing of the owl, together with the envelope in which it had been delivered, took what he told them.

They listened with courtesy and an air of mild interest, but that was just what Sergeant Wragg had done when Alistair had complained to him about the depredations and destructiveness of the youthful gangs from South Rollway. At the end of that interview the sergeant had promised to look into the matter, but had added that he didn't really think there was much he could do about the trouble unless Alistair caught one of the culprits redhanded and was ready to bring a charge against him.

He had spoken in a tone of resignation. It was as if he had known quite well that when it came to the point, Alistair would not bring a charge against a child, and considered, this being so, that he should perhaps not have wasted the sergeant's time with his complaint. However, that the manner of the police in Floxsted should be so like the sergeant's seemed to Alistair strange, until, thinking it over on his way back to the village, he began to wonder if he might not have misinterpreted it. The lack of surprise, the quiet taking of only a note or two, might not have meant lack of interest, but rather, knowledge. It might have meant that these men were already in possession of a good many of the facts about the murder in Monte Carlo and the Griffins that Alistair had given them.

Pondering what this in its turn might mean, he arrived home in time for the early lunch which had been planned so that he,

Rose and Irene could go up to the field in good time before the fête was to open. As he turned the car into the drive, Rose, who had spent most of the morning in the show-tent, helping with arrangements and setting up her own exhibit of sweet peas, was just wheeling a trolley, laid with a cold lunch, into the patch of shade under the cherry tree.

The day was as warm and bright as ever, the sky was cloudless, and the garden would have been a very peaceful spot except that someone on the field was experimenting with the loudspeaker that was to be used for announcements during the fête, sudden coughs and exclamations blaring out from time to time, punctuated by sundry whizz-ings and bangings.

Rose asked what had happened in Floxsted and Alistair told her, adding that he thought the police had probably been more interested than they had wanted him to know.

Rose glanced at her watch. 'Have you seen Irene?' she asked.

'No,' he said. 'Isn't she here?'

'She told me she was going for a walk, and she hasn't got back yet,' Rose replied. 'I rather think she's really gone to see Paul.'

'She's become very anxious all of a sudden to see him, after doing very well without him for a number of years,' Alistair said, sitting

150

down.

'I think she's very fond of him,' Rose said.

He glanced up at her quickly. She was arranging some plates on the trolley.

She went on, 'But she's rather afraid of him. I think she always was.'

'Afraid of Paul?' he said in protest. 'Irene?'

Rose hesitated, then said, 'I don't think you've ever known Paul very well. I sometimes feel afraid of him too. You see, he's a person who can go to extremes.'

From the field, the loudspeaker suddenly roared. 'Sorry, sorry—try that again?'

'Isn't that something we can all do, given provocation?' Alistair said.

'Oh, perhaps.'

'I'm sure Irene can go to extremes quite easily.'

'Yes, they've a lot in common, under the surface.' She turned towards the house. 'They ought to have stayed married to one another,' she added as she walked away.

Staring after her, it struck him that this was the first occasion, for a long time, that Rose had voluntarily mentioned Paul, and that what she had had to say about him was rather astonishing. Alistair had an impulse to get up and follow her, but just then Irene came in at the garden gate.

She had been hurrying and her face was

151

flushed, her breath coming quickly. Her first words, shrilly and violently spoken, showed that the cause of the colour and the panting was nearly all rage.

'Would you believe it?' she cried. 'Would you ever believe it? He wouldn't see me! I went there on purpose to be nice to the bastard. I went there determined to be my very, nicest self. I went there just so that he couldn't possibly be hurt because I hadn't been to see him, and I'd made up my mind that whatever he said or did I'd restrain myself and go on being nice. Nice! I tell you I was so nice I almost made myself sick. And what d'you think he did?'

'What?' Alistair asked with interest.

'Stood there in the doorway and told me he had an appointment!'

'That's all?'

'*All*?' She looked at him as if he had gone mad. 'I go there with tears in my eyes and my heart pinned on my sleeve and all he says is that he's got an *appointment*!'

'Perhaps he had one,' Alistair suggested.

'The only appointment he had was with his own damned self-righteousness,' Irene said. 'D'you know he wouldn't even let me into his house? And he said we could see each other this afternoon at this blasted fête I'm supposed to be opening—see each other in front of all those people! Can you imagine a worse insult?'

'I'm not really sure that I can,' Alistair said.

'No! And now let me tell you this,' Irene said. 'You're my friends, so it's only right I should warn you. I don't want trouble, I don't like trouble, it isn't my nature to make trouble. But I can't always count on myself. Sometimes when I've been very, very sorely tried, my temper gets a little out of hand and then I sometimes do things that I regret afterwards. And if Paul tries to sell me one of his miserable ices this afternoon, I don't promise not to plaster it all over his face. Or hit him over the head with one of his bottles of minerals. And neither of those things, believe me, will be half as bad as what he did to me this morning, standing there on his doorstep and saying politely—yes, God forgive him, he even said it *politely*—that he couldn't invite me in because he'd got an appointment!'

CHAPTER TEN

If it was in Irene's mind to assault her ex-husband with a bottle of fizzy lemonade, fate in one respect seemed to be playing straight into her hands, for by one of the usual errors that always produced last-minute drama on the day of the fête, only large-size bottles of minerals had been delivered, where only the small had been ordered.

The secretary, rushing up to welcome Irene, said almost tearfully to Rose and Alistair that she had had a most harrowing time getting anything delivered at all, and now, because it was so hot, people were already asking for drinks and ices, and she could not find Mr. Eckleston, who was supposed to be in charge of them. She said that she could not take them over herself, because in a few minutes she would have to start arranging the children's sports, and she asked Alistair whether, if the worst came to the worst—that was to say, if Mr. Eckleston did not arrive soon—he would take charge of Mr. Eckleston's stall.

Alistair agreed, then went to buy tickets from Henry, who was sitting at a card-table, just inside the gate of the field. The table was in the shade of an oak tree, but still Henry appeared to be suffering from the heat. His face was sallow and shiny with sweat, there were beads of sweat all over the bald crown of his head, and his eyes, behind the crooked spectacles, were bloodshot.

'Keep your tickets, won't you?' he said. 'Lucky numbers on them. Oh, Alistair, meant to ask you . . .' He leant forward over the rickety little table and dropped his voice. 'Those people who turned up yesterday at your house. The Griffins. Who on earth are they?'

'Just two people we met in the South of France,' Alistair answered.

Henry looked at him suspiciously. 'That's what I thought you said yesterday.'

'Why? Have they been bothering you?'

'Had them on my hands all the morning,' Henry answered. 'Pretended they wanted to see the Purslem. Raved about the pictures. Crazy to see the tapestries. In fact couldn't tell one thing from another, didn't care either, just wanted to ask questions.'

'What about?'

'You and Rose.' Henry broke off to sell tickets to a mother and four children who had just come in at the gate.

As they wandered off across the field, he went on, 'I know it's trouble of some sort about that business in Monte Carlo. Business

155

I got you into. Can't say how sorry I am. If only I'd used my head, I'd have smelt a rat straight away and never touched the proposition. Look, there they are now— over there by the show-tent. Came in a few minutes ago, asking if you were here.'

Alistair looked across the field.

It was already dotted with people, though the number, he thought, seemed to be greater than it was because of the way that most of the members of the committee were contriving to be in several places at the same time. The largest crowd was gathered around the entrance to the big marquee in which the fruit and flower exhibits had been set out and among them, conspicuous even at this distance, was the short figure of Mrs. Griffin, clothed in pink cotton, patterned with golden sunflowers.

'Well, if there's anything suspicious about them, at least there's nothing furtive,' Alistair said. 'One could hardly fail to observe her presence.'

'Can't see her husband,' Henry said, peering across the field. 'Came in with her. Must have gone in to look at the exhibits. Agnes is in there, by the way, selling raffle tickets. Must be perishing hot, but she seems to like that. Heat suits her. Rather feel it myself, doesn't agree with me. Yes, Mrs. McNiece?'

A young woman, looking hot and rumpled, had just come running across the field towards him, with three young children racing after her.

'Oh, Mr. Wallbank, have you seen Mr. Eckleston?' she gasped. 'If they don't start selling the ices soon, there's going to be a riot. I've been told they won't be on sale until the show's been opened by Miss Byrd, but young children can't understand that and actually I think they'd keep far quieter while she's talking if they'd something to occupy them.'

In their own fashion and at the tops of their voices, the three young McNieces endorsed what she had said.

Alistair said, 'I'm taking over if Mr. Eckleston doesn't show up. So I may as well start now.'

He had a word with Rose about it, to make sure that she felt that she could manage the Joy Wheel alone, then crossed the field to the point where a dense concentration of children showed him that the cases of ices and minerals had been deposited.

For the next quarter of an hour he was too busy to notice anything that happened on the field beyond the mass of children's faces, packed round him in a dense circle, the radius of which steadily extended as new arrivals poured in at the gate.

Irene's name on the posters appeared to have been as big an attraction as had been hoped. There were a great many television sets in South Rollway, and though its inhabitants normally participated very little in village affairs, to-day they were turning out in force, all the young members of each family rushing straight from the gate to Alistair's stall. Once their needs had been satisfied there, they looked challengingly round the field, then surged straight on to where Rose was setting out the little packets of sweets on the Joy Wheel. Just as the crowds of tourists in Monte Carlo had streamed up the steps of the Casino, so the children of South Rollway concentrated instantly on the best gamble in sight.

The chairman had taken charge of Irene. From somewhere he had managed to unearth an ancient farm-cart, painted in bright colours, to be her platform. She had dressed for her part in red. At least five different shades of red, Alistair thought, counting them. She had on a red sleeveless dress with a darker red belt and red shoes, she carried a red bag, and she had pinned a red rose at her throat. Her fair hair was brushed out on her shoulders.

She was nervous and kept scanning the crowd for Paul. Or so she said later. But during that hectic fifteen minutes before she stepped up on to the cart to declare the show open, both Alistair and Rose were far too busy to pay any attention to her. The chairman was busy coughing experimentally into the microphone that had been set up on the cart. Henry was busy at the gate. Agnes was busy inside the show-tent, selling raffle-tickets. In fact, for that little while, no one took much notice of Irene.

There was, besides all the desperate activity normal at that time, something else which distracted attention from her. Just as the microphone, which until then had been emitting small wheezing sounds, barely audible even to those who were gathered around the cart, startlingly sent one of the chairman's polite coughs roaring across the field, another sound made people suddenly lift their heads and listen.

Mr. Tolliver, contented with the first prize that he had won for his onions, nodded his head as if he had known it all along.

'Thunder,' he said.

Along the horizon a shape of an angry purple-grey was sliding up from behind the curving edge of the downs.

But this had happened more than once during the last few weeks and the rain fallen elsewhere. As Irene climbed on to the cart, and as the chairman, introducing her, began his little speech of welcome, the cloud in the sky seemed to be something of merely theatrical menace. That after so many weeks of drought, real rain might pour down on to the coatless, summery crowd and the parched field seemed hardly conceivable.

Irene said her piece very well. As she had promised, she told the people of Rollway what fine people they were. She told them what a fine village they lived in. She told them how much they were going to enjoy the fête and how much she enjoyed being there to enjoy it with them. While she was speaking, Alistair found his stall deserted and walked across to Rose.

'Can you manage without me, if Paul doesn't turn up?' he asked.

She nodded, giving the arrow at the centre of the wheel a spin and watching it till it stopped, pointing at a packet of fruit drops.

'What's kept him away, d'you think?' she asked. 'Irene?'

'It rather looks as if he found he couldn't face her,' Alistair answered.

'Yet you'd think he'd have telephoned somebody that he wasn't coming.'

He agreed and wandered on to have a word with Henry, who was doing very good business at the gate.

Henry surprised him by saying that Paul had arrived.

'Some minutes ago, I think,' Henry said. He peered vaguely towards the crowd gathered around the cart to listen to Irene, but people were packed too close together to make it easy to pick out any particular person. 'You haven't seen him?'

'No,' Alistair said.

'Didn't notice him particularly, just remember that he came in,' Henry said. 'Perhaps he's in the show-tent. Or perhaps he forgot something and went home again. Dare say I shouldn't have noticed him leave. Been too busy.'

Alistair nodded, and, realising that Irene was just coming to the end of her little speech, went back to his stall and got ready for more custom.

For the next half-hour or so, he was again very busy. If Paul had returned, he did not come to relieve Alistair. But probably, Alistair thought, he had not come back at all.

Out of the corner of his eye, he saw that Rose also was very busy. The Joy Wheel was a great attraction. So was Irene, selling her autograph and signed photographs of herself. From the far end of the field the amplified voice of the secretary, organising the children's sports, reached Alistair, punctuated

161

by the wooden clack, clack, from nearer at hand, of the ladies' and the gentlemen's bowling. Faces he knew, faces he half knew, appeared and reappeared near him as he handed out ice-creams, ice-lollies and bottles of minerals.

Meanwhile, the purplish grey patch of cloud, like a bruise coming out on the sky, slowly edged its way upwards. Thunder growled from time to time in the distance.

It was about an hour after the fête had been opened, when the supply of ices had almost run out and the secretary, hurrying by, looking distraught with all her responsibilities, said that someone must be despatched by car to pick up another consignment, that there was a sudden commotion around the Joy Wheel.

Squeals of excitement, louder than those that had already occurred whenever the arrow had stopped and some gratified child had clutched his packet of gums or peppermints or fruit drops, made Alistair turn his head to see what was happening.

At first he could make nothing of it, then he realised that Rose, standing back from the wheel and holding something clenched in one fist, was raising her voice over the shouting of the children to ask some question.

She was answered by what sounded, even

162

at that distance, like a chorus of denials. She asked the question again, pointing at a particular boy. He stood, for a moment, staring defiantly back at her, then took to his heels.

Alistair spoke hastily to a woman, standing nearby, asking her to keep an eye on his stall, then hurried over to Rose. She saw him coming and ran towards him.

'Look,' she said, opening the hand that she had been holding clenched, and showed him what lay on the palm of it.

He was half prepared for what he saw there. If certain thoughts had not been in the back of his mind for days past, it would certainly have taken him longer than it did to recognise what Rose was holding. The recognition was, of course, only partial. He could not actually identify the coin. But that it was something singular, something ancient, something perhaps precious, and by no means the kind of coin that could normally come out of the pockets of a boy from South Rollway, to be risked on a Joy Wheel, was plain at a glance.

Holding it, he said to Rose in a low voice, 'What happened?'

The coin was of silver and about the size of a half-crown. The design of a woman's head, a woman of severe but lovely profile, with close-curling hair, surrounded by some fishlike creatures, seemed to him very beautiful.

'I don't know exactly,' she said. 'There was a crowd of children round the wheel and I'd just set out a new set of sweets on it and they'd been putting their pennies on. Then just as I was going to spin the thing, something distracted my attention. I looked away and I suppose that's when it happened. I mean, that's when one of them pocketed one of the pennies and put this down instead.'

'Do you remember what it was that distracted your attention?'

'Yes, one of the children shouted and pointed away over the field.'

'And was there anything to look at there?'

'Not particularly.'

'So there was more than one of them in it. That boy who ran off—who was he?'

'I don't know. I mean I don't know his name, though I think I've seen him about. He's one of the gang from South Rollway.'

'Why did he run off?'

'Because as soon as I saw this thing and asked who'd put it there, the other children all yelled, 'He done it!'

'But he wasn't the one who shouted and pointed?'

'No.'

'Do you remember which one that was?'

Rose looked back towards the corner of the

field where the Joy Wheel stood. There was still a crowd of children around it, but there had been some change in them. Instead of being packed closely around the table, intent on the game, they were in groups of three or four, a pace or two away from the table, with an air of waiting and watching, half furtively, half in excitement, for trouble to break out.

'It was a girl, I think,' Rose said. 'I think it was the one with the blue ribbons in her hair.'

Alistair walked towards the little knot of children.

Going at his side, Rose said, 'This is the same as the letter, isn't it? Someone's trying to scare us, or make some sort of horrible fun of us.'

'That's how it looks.'

'Those Griffins.'

'Probably.'

'She's over there now,' Rose said, nodding towards the tea-tent. 'I haven't seen him all the afternoon.'

'No. Well, let's see what we can get out of this girl,' Alistair said.

The girl was about ten, tall for her age and pretty, with curly dark hair cut in a fringe across her forehead and tied with a blue bow on each temple. She had on a fresh-looking blue and white striped cotton dress and carried a little white plastic handbag.

She was older than most of the children standing near her and as she saw Alistair approach, she assumed a responsible air of conscious virtue.

'I don't know nothing about it,' she said before Alistair had spoken to her.

'What's your name?' he asked.

'Jessica,' she answered.

'Jessica what?'

'Jessica Boley.'

'And that boy who ran off just now—what's his name?'

'Ted.'

'Ted what?'

'That's my brother Ted.'

'Oh, so your brother told you to shout suddenly and point at something on the other side of the field, while he changed the coins on the wheel?'

'I don't know nothing about why he wanted me to do it,' she said. 'And he didn't mean no harm, it was just a joke.'

'That's right, mister,' another child piped up. 'He didn't take no sweets nor nothing.'

'That's right,' Jessica Boley said. 'And when they wanted to pinch the sweets when Mrs. Dirke run off I said they wasn't to. I said, "Don't you touch," I said, "they aren't yours"—didn't I?' she appealed to her

166

witnesses.

'That's right,' they chorused.

'Ted just done it for a joke,' Jessica repeated.

Alistair nodded. 'Yes, of course it was just a joke. But what I'd like to know is who gave this coin to your brother and told him to put it on the wheel. Because I expect whoever it was wants the coin back.'

'They never said nothing about wanting it back, they just said—' Jessica broke off, realising that she was admitting more knowledge than she had intended. 'It's just an old foreign coin anyway, it isn't any good. The lady said it wasn't any good. She said we couldn't buy ice-creams with it, or anything like that. But you could try putting it on the wheel over there, she said, when nobody's looking. That'd be different, she said. It's a lucky piece, she said, perhaps you'll have luck with it. And she gave Ted a couple of bob to do it.'

'A lucky piece *and* two bob!' Alistair said. 'That sounds like Ted's lucky day.'

'Only we didn't have no luck with it,' Jessica said quickly, as if this fact might help to absolve her and her brother from any guilt that might turn out to have attended the transaction.

'She was the same lady, I suppose,' Alistair

said, 'who paid your brother a few days ago to deliver a letter to our house.'

He saw the flare of fright in the girl's eyes. The simple act of putting two and two together seemed to strike her as uncanny.

'I don't know nothing about it,' she muttered.

'Wasn't it a short stout lady, with a lot of beads round her neck?'

'That's right—a foreign lady.'

'Foreign?' he said in surprise.

'That's right.'

'What makes you think she was foreign?'

'She and the gentleman talked foreign to each other.'

'What language—?' he began, but realised that that was not a question that a child from South Rollway was likely to be able to answer. 'She and her husband talked a foreign language to each other, so that you and your brother shouldn't be able to understand what they were talking about, is that it?' he suggested.

'Maybe,' she said.

'And that's the lady . . .' He had turned and had been about to point at Mrs. Griffin, standing outside the tea-tent, when, as he looked towards the point where he had seen her a few moments before, he realised that she was no longer visible.

168

Glancing about the field, he could not see her anywhere else either.

'Well, never mind,' he said. 'But for the present, I'm going to keep this coin. Tell your brother, if he wants it back, to come and see me.'

Thrusting his hand, with the coin held in it, into his pocket, he walked away.

Rose went a little way after him.

'What are you going to do now?' she asked. 'I can't come with you till I've got someone to take charge of the wheel.'

'I'm going to talk to Harry,' he said. 'I want to know exactly what this thing is.'

She gave him one of the looks which he was coming to associate with any mention by him of Henry. It was as if it were beyond her to forgive Henry for what he had involved them in. But she did not argue this time against taking him into their confidence.

'Wait for me,' she said, and ran off to find someone who would look after the Joy Wheel.

While Alistair waited for her, the first rain-drops fell.

But at that time only a few fell, large and cool and widely scattered, so that people began to argue as to whether or not it was actually raining. Many insisted that it was not. But here and there, where the drops had

169

fallen on bare earth, from which the grass had shrivelled away during the drought, they left little round damp dents which could be pointed at as almost marvellous proof that rain could fall.

Rose came running back and she and Alistair went to speak to Henry.

He was still sitting at the card table at the gate, but his trade had dropped off. More people were leaving the field now than were coming in. He was leaning back on his rickety chair, wonderingly wiping the top of his head with his handkerchief.

'Rain,' he remarked, after he had looked hard at the handkerchief, reassuring himself, it seemed, that it was not some more sinister sort of moisture that had fallen on his head. 'Going to come down in buckets any minute, I shouldn't wonder.'

'Henry,' Alistair said, taking his hand out of his pocket and holding it out, 'do you know what this is?'

Henry looked, stared, and lurched to his feet. One of his hands shot out to grasp Alistair by the wrist.

'Where did you get that?' he shouted.

Without thinking, instinctively, Alistair wrenched his wrist free.

Henry shouted something else at him. But whatever it was, the words were lost in the crash of thunder, that seemed to come at the same moment as a blinding flash of lightning, and that sounded like the crack of a great whip just above their heads.

Then down came the rain, beating on to them out of the blackened sky, as the cloud emptied itself in a hissing torrent on to the field.

CHAPTER ELEVEN

They were wet through before they reached the shelter of the show-tent. Caught in the entrance in a wave of other people, all struggling to get out of the rain, Alistair lost sight of Henry. But once inside, he saw him again, bending over the table at which Agnes was seated, selling raffle tickets. As Henry talked swiftly into her ear, her gaze swept the crowd until it lighted on Alistair, and she beckoned excitedly. But a solid mass of hot, wet humanity barred the way to her. Nodding back, to show that he would come when he could, he let the pressure of the crowd carry him farther into the tent.

By linking her arm through his, Rose managed to stay with him. She seemed to be tugging him towards the long tables on which the flower exhibits had been set out. Though he had not yet looked at these, he was in no mood to do so now, and was about to say so when he realised that Rose's goal was not the vase of splendid gladioli sent along by the vicar's wife, but was Mrs. Griffin, held prisoner just in front of the vase by a hedge of elbows.

When she saw Rose and Alistair coming,

she smiled as widely as she had smiled at them on the beach at Cap Martin. Just as, on the beach, she had always been loaded with an extraordinary number of books, cushions and lotions, so now she was clasping in her plump arms an amazing collection of parcels and prizes. It was evident that she had been to all the stalls and side-shows and spent money freely.

The sight of her standing there had a curious effect on Alistair. It was an effect at the same time of familiarity and of strangeness. Yet it was the smile, which should have been familiar, that was strange, for there was something about it that seemed fixed and false, while the feeling of familiarity came from something in her eyes that he could not identify. But intensely, for a moment, he had the sensation of this having happened to him before, of having once before met her eyes with just that expression of wariness and suspicion in them.

He thought of the afternoon when he had seen her and her husband in the Casino. But that was not it, for it was the relationship between her and himself, created by the look in the suspicious eyes, that was familiar.

But that was nonsense. There had been no such relationship before.

When he and Rose were near enough, Mrs.

Griffin called out to them, 'What a pity, what a pity—just when it was all going so well!'

She was, of course, referring to the fête and the way that it had been spoilt by the rain, but Alistair decided to read another meaning into her words.

'You must have known what would happen,' he said.

She wrinkled her forehead at him. 'Known. . . ?'

'That it wouldn't be hard for us to guess who was behind it.'

'Behind it?' she said vacantly.

'Behind the letter, behind the way that coin, whatever it is, appeared on the Joy Wheel.'

She gave a gay little giggle. 'Oh, did the little boy really use it for that? How sweet!' she cried.

In the hot, sodden atmosphere of the tent, which had somehow transformed the delicate, fresh scents of the garden flowers into a heavy and cloying cloud, Alistair suddenly felt the choking sensation of an almost insane anger.

'I tell you, we know what you've been up to!' he shouted at her. 'We don't know why, or what you've got against us, but we know you're trying to threaten and intimidate us.'

'But, Professor Dirke—'

'Didn't you expect us to realise that, as soon as you showed yourselves at our house yesterday?' he raged, indifferent to the fact that a number of faces in the crowd around him had just turned towards him, bright with the hope of unexpected diversion. 'You're trying for some reason to entangle my wife and me in that atrocious business in Monte Carlo. But all you've achieved so far is to underline your own connection with it. It may interest you to know that this morning I took your letter to the police.'

He thought her soft, wrinkled face tightened slightly, but he was too angry to be sure.

'It hadn't escaped our notice that you vanished from Cap Martin on the night of the murder!' he ranted.

But as soon as he had spoken that word, he regretted it, and Rose's hand, tightening on his arm, told him that she also considered it a mistake.

She spoke quietly to Mrs. Griffin. 'You could have approached us without all the hocus-pocus, couldn't you? If you had questions to ask us, why couldn't you simply ask them?'

'I simply don't know what either of you is talking about,' Mrs. Griffin said. 'All because I gave a little boy who was standing there a lucky charm that had come off my bracelet.

He picked it up for me, and I thought that was so sweet of him, I told him to keep it and gave him two shillings as a reward for his honesty. And this turns into something to do with a murder!'

Alistair thought that her answer was about as inane as it could have been, but he glanced once more at the coin that he still held clenched in his hand, and saw now that it had a small hole, punched through the metal close to the rim.

'Oh yes,' Mrs. Griffin said, seeing him regarding this, 'it really did come off my bracelet.' And she held up her wrist, round which she was wearing a band of silver links, from which dangled a number of jingling silver objects. She showed him the space where one had been broken off. 'My husband gave it to me for my birthday,' she said.

Oddly enough, that innocent-sounding remark cleared the fog from Alistair's mind. He stared at her hard. He knew now why she had looked familiar to him.

'Oh, your *husband* gave it to you,' he said, in a tone of confirming, not of questioning what she had said.

It was a tone that seemed to alarm her. She started to edge away from him.

'My dear,' she said to Rose, 'your clever husband's too much for me. You may be able to manage him, but my husband and I, we're quite simple people. I wish, I really do wish, that we'd never dropped in on you. But how can one know about things like that in advance? We'd remembered you as such charming and friendly people. But, of course, people are never the same on holiday as they are at home, and we shouldn't have counted on your being pleased to see us.'

Rose's tone was quieter than Alistair's, but no warmer. 'Where's your husband now, Mrs. Griffin? I haven't seen him all the afternoon.'

'Oh, he came here with me,' Mrs. Griffin said, 'but then he decided to go back to our hotel. I don't think village fêtes are really much in his line. Now I just love them. I've had a simply lovely time, particularly chatting to that lovely girl. . . . Oh, there she is—excuse me!' And with a violent movement, which resulted in a jar of home-made jam being knocked out of her arms and falling to the ground with a crunch of breaking glass, she thrust her way into the crowd, battering a passage through it towards Irene.

Somehow managing to look cool and sweet, even in five shades of red and the heat of the tent, Irene was still signing autographs. But there was a glazed look in her eyes, as if she were doing it in a dream.

Alistair turned to Rose.

'Let's go back to Henry and find out what this thing really is,' he said.

She grasped his arm again and together they worked their way back towards the entrance of the tent.

Seen through the opening, the rain looked like a sheet of steel, chill and solid. Wherever the ground had been trodden hard by the crowds, wide brown puddles had already formed. A few hardy souls were walking away through the downpour and others near the entrance were muttering that that was what they might as well do, since it was clear that the rain would go on for hours. The crashes of thunder were still very loud.

Before reaching Henry and Agnes, who were still at their table, Rose and Alistair encountered the vicar, who was looking gloomily out at the field, his hair plastered down to his scalp by the rain and his shirt clinging wetly to his shoulders.

'Well, well, a disappointing day, but we mustn't grumble,' he said.

Alistair's anger, roused by Mrs. Griffin's tricks and obvious lies, had by no means subsided. 'I'll grumble all I want to,' he answered with a fierceness that made the vicar say in a disturbed tone, 'But it's needed, you know. The country needs it. The water situation in Manchester is really serious.'

'You don't imagine it's raining in Manchester!' Alistair said bitterly, and thrust his way on towards Henry, leaving the vicar, who plainly found such an absence of resignation about the weather strange, perhaps shocking and even downright un-English, looking after him with raised eyebrows.

'Well?' Alistair said to Henry.

Agnes answered, 'No, no, we can't talk about it here, can we? If there's anything to talk about, because I can't make head or tail of what Henry's been telling me. One or other of you seems to me to have gone clean out of his mind. Or both of you. Rose—' She appealed to her. 'I know Henry's nerves are in a shocking state and the heat upsets him, and Alistair's a professor. But you—you don't think this can be true, do you?'

'I don't know what Henry's told you,' Rose said.

'No,' Henry said. 'Didn't have time out there. But we can't talk here, Agnes is right.'

'Let's go home, then,' Alistair said.

'But the rain—'

'Our car's out there.'

'Be soaked before we get there. Don't mind for myself. Wet already. But can't have Agnes catching cold.'

'Look,' Alistair said, 'we've got to talk this

thing over. So I'll go out there and get the car and drive it up here. Agnes will have three or four yards to run through the rain. Will that suit you?'

'You can't drive a car on to the field.'

'It's what I'm going to do.'

'But if you do, so will everyone else.'

'Let them!'

Thrusting between two pairs of shoulders that were blocking his way, Alistair plunged out into the rain.

The scowl on his face when, a few minutes later, he drove his car straight back across the field to the tent, caused several people to look at him in surprise. Henry and Agnes, leaping across a wide puddle and bundling into the back of the car, looked startled and uneasy, rather as if they felt that they were accepting a lift from a possibly dangerous stranger, while Rose, following them out of the tent and slipping quickly into the seat beside Alistair, gave him a swift glance, then stared straight ahead through the streaming windscreen.

He was just about to drive off when the secretary came running out to them.

'You'll be back, won't you?' she cried. 'The show isn't over. And even if it is, there's all the clearing up to do. I can't manage that by myself and I don't see why it should be expected of me either. I don't mind doing my share, but there comes a point—'

'We'll be back,' Alistair said, and sent the car forward.

He drove straight home. Henry, in the back seat, made one or two muttering remarks, and once Agnes gave an excited laugh, but neither Rose nor Alistair spoke until they had reached the house. As they went into the sitting-room, Rose said that she would make some tea and disappeared into the kitchen to put the kettle on, but almost immediately she returned and instead of sitting down, stood still in the middle of the room, looking round her in a puzzled way, as if the place had suddenly become unfamiliar to her.

At the time Alistair, engrossed in what he had started to say to Henry, did not take much notice of this.

'Here,' he was saying to Henry as Rose came in, 'take a look at it and tell me what it is. Then I'll tell you where I got it. Then we can talk over what we'd better do about it.'

He held his hand out towards Henry, with the coin on his palm.

Henry reached out and took it gingerly. Straightening his spectacles, he brought the coin close to his eyes, blinked at it, then felt in a pocket and brought out a magnifying-glass.

As he looked at the coin through the magnifying-glass, the whole cast of his face seemed to alter. All the uncertainty and vague diffidence disappeared. Behind the spectacles that had already tilted slightly to one side, the eyes grew keen, the muscles of the cheeks taut, the mouth firm.

Alistair, who had seen this happen before, knew what it meant. It meant that Henry the expert, the enthusiast who knew what he was talking about, had taken control of the situation.

Agnes, who was gazing at Henry's face, and not, as might have been expected, at the coin, gave a little gasp, as if this transformation, to which by now, it might be thought, she would be accustomed, still startled and stirred her.

'Fantastic,' Henry said. Even his voice seemed different. 'Been saying to myself all the way here it couldn't turn out to be true. Only saw it for a moment, after all, so I might have been seeing things.'

'That's what I said,' Agnes said. 'You've got the things so much on your mind—that's what I said—you just deceived yourself. What Alistair showed you was probably only a nickel or a mark or something.'

'Dear me, no!' Henry said, shaking his

head.

'Is it something very valuable, then?' Alistair asked.

'Oh, no, it isn't valuable,' Henry answered, as if the point were not of much interest. 'Would have been, of course, if it hadn't been ruined. The way it's been polished up—the hole drilled through it—vandalism. Got about as much value now as any other bit of fashionable jewellery. But if you mean what it *once* had . . .'

'Well?' Alistair said.

'You see,' Henry said, 'it's a silver decadrachm of Syracuse. Doesn't mean anything to you, I suppose? Well, it was minted about the year 400 B.C. Yes, it's more than two thousand years old. Makes you think, eh?'

'That's something I never can understand,' Agnes said. 'I mean why a thing just being old should make you think.'

'Ah, this isn't only old,' Henry said gently, but the gentleness was not for his wife, it was for the thing that he was holding. 'Look at this head of Persephone. Beautiful. By the artist Kimon. One of the most famous coins in existence—not excessively rare, actually, but quite, quite beautiful. Would have been, that's to say, in proper condition. Crime, what's been done to it. I'd hardly believe it if I didn't know. . . .' He paused, as if he had

183

said something that he had not intended to say.

'What do you know about it, Henry?' Alistair asked.

Henry's hand closed on the coin. As he looked up at Alistair, the customary uncertainty was back in his eyes.

'It's really just a guess, can't say I *know*,' he said. 'You haven't told me yet how in the world you got hold of it. But I told you, didn't I, that Pantelaras and his wife had separated before he ever came over here, and that one day he told me something about the business and that I had a good deal of sympathy with him? Did tell you that, didn't I, the day we sat out in your garden and I persuaded you to take on the job of going to see him? Well, this coin—I mean, if this is the coin I think it is—was the reason they separated.'

'You mean this coin belonged to Pantelaras?' Alistair said.

'One of the gems of his collection,' Henry answered. 'One of the best things in it. Worth—oh, say, fifteen hundred pounds, *à fleur de coin*—in mint condition, that is—as it was then. But his wife didn't care about his collection, you see. Thought he spent too much money on it. Always quarrelling about it. Wanted him to sell it. Yes, actually. Well,

184

can't say I haven't some sympathy with her too. Wanted her daughter to have a good chance in life, and all that—perfectly natural. But to Pantelaras it would have been the end of his life. Yes, I really believe without his collection to think and dream about he'd just have packed up and died. And I suppose he tried to make her understand that. And so one day she goes and takes this coin—he kept his collection at home in those days, not at the bank—and she takes it to a jeweller and gets him to punch a hole in it and has it hung on a bracelet.' Henry gave a dry laugh. 'Well, that was the end of their marriage.'

'I see. So when this coin was last heard of, it was in the possession of Mrs. Pantelaras?'

'If it's the same coin,' Henry said. 'But that two specimens of this particular coin should have had the same fate would be queer, eh? Too much of a coincidence. Now tell me, where did you get it?'

'One of the children from South Rollway dumped it down on the Joy Wheel instead of a penny,' Alistair said.

Henry stared at him in disbelief, while Agnes gave one of her terrible whoops of laughter.

'It's perfectly true,' Alistair said. 'It was a boy called Boley, with a sister called Jessica.'

'Alistair,' Rose said softly at that point,

'there's something I think I ought to tell you. Like Henry, I've been trying to make up my mind whether or not I was seeing things. Because the fact is that nothing in this room is quite in the position that it was in when we went out after lunch. That vase there, my work-basket, the chair-covers, those books . . .'

She pointed at each item as she named it, then looked at Alistair.

'And it's the same in the kitchen,' she said, 'and I shouldn't be surprised to find it was the same in all the other rooms. Because I think what it means is that while we were at the fête, someone got into this house and searched it from top to bottom.'

CHAPTER TWELVE

There was a silence as Alistair, Henry and Agnes looked round the room.

Then Agnes spoke collectedly. 'That's something, of course, that you would know, Rose.'

'Yes,' Rose said. 'Things have their proper places. Our charwoman thinks so too, though she doesn't quite agree with me about it, so when she leaves I usually go round and put things back where I think they belong. I did that this morning. And as soon as we came in, I noticed that everything was just a little out of place again.'

'And you think that means the house has been searched?' Alistair said.

'Doesn't it? And I think we can guess who did it,' she said.

'Griffin?'

Henry exclaimed, 'Why on earth Griffin? I don't understand this.'

'Because Mrs. Griffin is the ex-Mrs. Pantelaras,' Alistair said. 'I realised that in the tent and it makes a certain sense of what's been happening. This coin—' He reached out to take it from Henry, who let him do so with a shade of reluctance. 'This coin came off a bracelet that Mrs. Griffin is wearing.'

Agnes looked at him searchingly. Suddenly he realised what Rose had meant when she said that Agnes, when she chose, was an acute, intelligent woman.

'But you didn't know anything about the coin having belonged to Mrs. Pantelaras when you were in the tent, did you, Alistair? Or did you?' she asked.

'No, not a thing,' he said. 'But when I first caught sight of her there in the tent, I suppose taking her by surprise, she forgot to try to look as if I were her dear old friend, and showed all her suspicion of me. And then I recognised her, as well as understanding something else that had puzzled me quite a bit in Monte Carlo.' He turned to Rose. 'You remember what I told you about Madame Robinet—that when I first saw her I felt sure I'd seen her before? And then I became sure I hadn't. Well, what I'd really seen in that first glance, was her likeness to her mother whom we'd been seeing every day at the pension. They're both small, plump, dark-eyed, dark-haired women, though Mrs. Griffin's gone grey now. And when they've the same sort of expression on their faces—that sharp, startled, suspicious look—there's simply no mistaking the relationship.'

'But why have they come *here*?' Henry

188

demanded helplessly.

Agnes answered, 'To recover the collection from that bloodstained murderer, Professor Dirke!' She began to laugh again. 'Oh dear, oh dear, things are so funny sometimes. Imagine their thinking such a thing! Though it's easy to see how they worked it out.'

'I don't think it's funny at all,' Henry muttered.

'What are you going to do about it, Alistair?' Agnes asked.

'Have a talk with them,' he answered.

'What, now?'

'Yes, now. Want to come?'

'But we ought to go back to the field,' Henry said. 'Look, the rain's stopped.'

Alistair had been far too engrossed to give a thought to the weather. Now, in a glance at the window, he saw that a faint golden light was shining in a watery-looking but clear sky. A blackbird was singing exultantly in the cherry tree.

'I'll take you and Agnes back to the field, if you like,' he said, 'and offer Mrs. Griffin a lift back to her hotel in Floxsted, where I think we'll find her husband.'

'You aren't coming back to help, then?' Henry said, as if this development confused him even further. 'You said you'd be back.'

'I didn't know then that we'd had a

burglar. I think,' Alistair said, glancing questioningly at Rose, 'our burglar gets priority.'

She nodded and said, 'I'll come with you.'

'I don't know—I'd like to come,' Henry said. 'Be very interesting, but . . .'

Agnes shook her head decisively. A little to Alistair's surprise, but to his distinct relief, she said, 'We can go back to the field to help.'

So it was without the Wallbanks that Alistair and Rose presently drove to Floxsted, after dropping Henry and Agnes at the entrance to the field, looking around for Mrs. Griffin and failing to find her. Supposing that she had probably set off for Floxsted ahead of them, they drove straight on to the town.

The storm still grumbled in the distance and the road was shiny with puddles, but the rain was at an end. Sunshine slanted into Alistair's eyes as he drove.

Half-way to Floxsted, Rose observed, 'Paul never came, did he?'

'Henry said he did,' Alistair answered.

'I didn't see him.'

'He must have left again almost at once.'

'As Mr. Griffin did. I wonder. . . .'

'What?'

'If that could be why Paul left.'

Alistair could make no sense of this. To the best of his belief, Paul and the Griffins had never even met.

'I should think the simple fact is that he got to the field, caught sight of Irene, and decided it was more than he could bear,' he said, wondering, as he spoke, whether it might not in fact have been Rose whom Paul had felt an imperative need to avoid. 'Talking of Irene, we've been forgetting all about her.'

'I looked around for her on the field just now,' Rose said. 'I didn't see her.'

'Perhaps she's gone to look for Paul.'

'I hope not.'

'Why?'

'I told you, you don't understand Paul,' she said.

That silenced him abruptly.

The Red Lion in Floxsted, the hotel at which the Griffins had said that they were staying, was the main hotel of the town, an old inn overlooking the market-place, modernised into a condition of dim and comfortless gentility. From the dead silence in it, as Rose and Alistair entered, it might have been thought, not only that there was nobody staying there, but that such service as was provided was invisible and soundless, as in some dreaming, enchanted palace. The striking of a little brass bell on a mahogany counter labelled 'Inquiries,' produced a little tinkling sound that died away as if it had never been.

Alistair reached for the bell and struck it again, and then again and again, more and more violently. He was in the kind of mood in which he felt that the whole world must be in a conspiracy to enrage him. Any small and accidental frustration felt like a calculated addition to the real cause for anger. When a small rabbit of a woman bolted out of a door marked 'Private,' and asked him, in a startled and offended tone, what he wanted, it was all that he could do to remember that almost certainly she had no connection whatever with the murder of Nikolo Pantelaras.

He told her that he wanted Mr. and Mrs. Griffin and she replied that no doubt they were having tea in the residents' lounge. Her tone implied that there was nothing else that they could be doing at that time of day. Waving vaguely at the staircase, she scuttled back into her office and shut the door quickly. Rose and Alistair started up the stairs.

They discovered the residents' lounge on the first floor. It was a big room with windows overlooking the street. At a little table in one of the windows, Mr. and Mrs. Griffin were sitting, eating some hotel-type fruit cake and whispering together, as if they felt that it would be an impropriety to break the silence of the big, dreary, empty room. They were

192

both watching the door expectantly, and Alistair realised that they must have seen him drive up to the hotel.

On seeing him and Rose, Mr. Griffin stood up, while Mrs. Griffin waved a bare arm, on which the silver charm-bracelet tinkled.

'Now isn't this nice?' she cried. 'You've come here to save us the trouble of coming to find you. How kind, how very kind.'

The atmosphere, as it always had been with the Griffins, except for those few minutes in the show-tent, seemed gay and friendly.

Mr. Griffin pulled a chair forward for Rose.

'We were coming to see you as soon as we'd had tea,' he said. 'Now may I ring for tea for you?'

'No, thank you,' Alistair said.

'No? It does, of course, take a very long time to arrive, but our experience is that it comes in the end. You're sure you won't have some?'

'No.'

'You prefer not to drink even tea with the enemy?'

'I want to know why you've decided to be the enemy,' Alistair said. 'Also I want to know why you've been searching our house.'

'Well, do at least sit down,' Mr. Griffin

193

said. 'We have a good deal to talk over.'

As Rose and Alistair stiffly accepted the chairs he indicated, he sat down himself, picked up his cup and held it out to his wife. Refilling it, she slopped some tea into the saucer and scolded herself softly. In spite of her smiling face, the plump hand holding the teapot had not been steady.

She seemed prepared to let her husband do the talking, which from the start gave a turn to the interview for which Alistair had not been prepared. Before, it had always been Mrs. Griffin who talked most, talked so much, indeed, that it left almost no room in any conversation for her husband to add more than an occasional monosyllable. Now she sat back with a fixed imitation of her usual smile on her face, while her dark eyes darted from one face to another.

'As to your being the enemy,' Mr. Griffin said, 'I'm not sure that I've ever considered you in that light.'

He drank some tea. His hands were perfectly steady and his eyes were grim. Remembering the glimpse of him in the Casino at Monte Carlo, the glimpse that at the time had seemed amusing, even though it had revealed something rather surprising in the quiet little manufacturer of toys, Alistair knew that it was not the ex-Mrs. Pantelaras with whom he had to deal now.

'You're in the habit, then, of searching the houses of your friends for stolen collections of coins?' Alistair's voice was harsh, though he had decided that in dealing with this small, dry man, whom hitherto he had written off as a mere obedient husband, a dutiful and unobtrusive breadwinner, it would not help him to let too much anger show. 'Also of sending anonymous letters?'

Mr. Griffin put his head consideringly on one side.

'No, I believe I've never done either thing before,' he said.

'You don't deny that you've done them now?'

'Would you believe me if I did?'

'No.'

'Well then.' Mr. Griffin spread his hands in a way that implied that he thought Alistair had asked a foolish question. 'But I'm prepared to offer you my heartfelt apologies.'

Mrs. Griffin gave an agitated bounce in her chair. 'Please be careful what you say, Bill.'

'Of course, my dear,' he replied. 'But we certainly owe Professor and Mrs. Dirke our apologies. They have every right to be very angry with us.'

Mrs. Griffin turned impulsively to Rose. 'But I mean to say, dear, you were right there

195

on the spot, weren't you? I mean in Monte Carlo. And there didn't seem to be any real reason why you should be.'

Rose did not actually stir, but she gave the impression of withdrawing herself from Mrs. Griffin.

'You were there too,' she said.

'We had the best of reasons for being there,' Mr. Griffin said.

'To visit Mrs. Griffin's daughter?' Alistair asked. 'But the secrecy with which you appear to have done that most natural thing is about the most suspicious circumstance of the whole lot.'

'There you are!' Mrs. Griffin exclaimed to her husband. 'You see, they do know too much. There's something wrong about it.'

He shook his head, not to contradict her, but to silence her.

'I'm going to tell you our story, Professor Dirke,' he said, 'and explain why we came here to see you. Since you've discovered my wife's relationship with Marie Robinet, I can make it shorter than I'd expected. I need hardly tell you, for instance, that our main object is to have Armand Robinet cleared of the false charge of murder.'

'In that case, you're surely wasting time in coming to Rollway,' Alistair said.

'Not if by doing so we can clear our minds

of certain doubts and suspicions.'

'By searching our house?'

Mr. Griffin gave a regretful smile. 'I can see that isn't going to be forgiven us. Well, that's natural. I know my own feelings of righteous indignation when a customs officer delves into a suitcase of mine. The sense of having one's intimate possessions scrutinised by a total stranger, rouses very atavistic instincts.'

'Since the customs officer is only doing his job,' Alistair said, 'which is strictly on the side of the law, I don't think the analogy is a good one.'

Rose's hands, lying on the arms of her chair, clenched suddenly. It was only a small movement, but it revealed an extreme of tension and impatience.

Mr. Griffin gave her a thoughtful look and went on, 'Well, as I was about to tell you, our reason for being in the South of France was directly connected with your presence there. Perhaps you've realised that. As soon as she learnt you were expected, my step-daughter wrote and implored us to come out and do what we could to help her. Her hope, of course, was to find some way of preventing her father's collection of coins, into which he'd sunk all the money which a more normal father would have kept for his family, from

197

being given away. I might add here, I think, that Armand is a sculptor. I know remarkably little about such things, but I've been assured by people who claim, at least, that they know a great deal, that he has promise. More importantly, Marie believes it. Marie believes that he ought to have a chance to develop his talent. You've no doubt heard of such wives. I admire her for it myself, though I think it's a hundred to one chance that she's a fool, particularly since, as it happens, she's expecting a baby. But there it is, he's her husband, and as I said, I admire her. And I think that that ten or eleven thousand pounds locked up in her father's collection ought to have gone to her.'

A look of challenge came into the eyes that steadily regarded Alistair.

'It may be that you don't think that important,' Mr. Griffin went on. 'I know nothing about your means and it may be that you think such a sum insignificant. If so, in these days you're a very lucky man. But I know that with the best will in the world, my wife and I can't help Marie to anything like that extent while we have to maintain ourselves.'

'Yes, but—' Alistair said and floundered. The accusation that he might be a rich enough man to think ten or eleven thousand pounds a mere nothing so confounded him for a moment that he could not think what it was that, at an earlier point in Mr. Griffin's speech, he had been about to say.

'Yes, but,' he said at last, 'Mr. Pantelaras wasn't *giving* that collection away to the Purslem. He was asking six thousand pounds for it.'

'I'm afraid I don't understand you,' Mr. Griffin said. 'Why do you mention that sum?'

'It's the price Mr. Pantelaras was asking for his collection,' Alistair said.

Mr. Griffin shook his head. 'He wasn't asking anything. The collection was to be a free gift to the Purslem. That was his way of taking revenge on Marie for her marriage. He disapproved of it and tried to prevent it, as he disapproved of and tried to prevent almost everything the poor girl did.'

'You've been misinformed,' Alistair said. 'Mr. Pantelaras was asking six thousand pounds for his collection. I suppose, since it was worth far more than that, it might, figuratively speaking, be called a gift, but I want it clear, for the purposes of this discussion, that it wasn't actually a gift. If it had been, I'm sure Mr. Wallbank would have accepted it on the spot, without asking me to call on Mr. Pantelaras to find out if there were any strings attached to the deal. Mr. Wallbank knew the collection already, and knew that

199

even at six thousand it was something to be jumped at.'

'So that's what you were supposed to be doing there,' Mr. Griffin said. 'Nevertheless, Pantelaras told his daughter that he was giving his collection away for nothing.'

'He told Mr. Wallbank that he wanted six thousand pounds for it.'

'This appears to be a deadlock.'

Alistair agreed that it was.

It was Mrs. Griffin, whose darting eyes had kept moving from one face to the other, as if she were watching a tennis match, who suggested a solution.

'All it means, you know, is that Nikolo was telling different stories to Marie and to Mr. Wallbank. I don't know what he was up to, but it's plain he'd got some trick up his sleeve, some little bit of dirty work—over and above, I mean, making Marie suffer.'

'Yes, but why—?' her husband began, meeting Alistair's watchful look with suspicious perplexity. Then he shrugged his shoulders. 'To proceed from that point,' he said, 'and reminding you that all our actions were based on the assumption that Pantelaras was giving his collection away for nothing, to spite Marie and her husband, we decided that we would do what we could to help her, and so went to Monte Carlo and took a room in the same pension as yourselves at Cap Martin. Our object was to become sufficiently friendly with you to be able to talk to you freely and explain the family situation. The fact is, we couldn't think of anything else to do. Marie had already looked into the possibility of persuading the *Conservateur en chef* of the *Cabinet des Medailles* to prevent the collection going abroad, but she wasn't hopeful about the results. I wasn't particularly hopeful about our plan either, but my wife, on getting to know you, said she was sure you would at least listen to us.'

He gave a little twitching smile.

'And you *are* listening—I admit that. But meanwhile Pantelaras has been murdered, and the coins have disappeared. And Armand Robinet is under arrest, charged with the murder. And it's a regrettable fact that on the evening of the murder, when he was questioned by the police, he completely lost his head, told a number of lies and omitted to mention one or two things that might have helped him.'

'The lies,' Alistair said, 'concerned his having been in the house. He denied it, although his fingerprints were all over the place. But now he's changed his story, confessed that he'd been there to try to reason with his father-in-law, found the door

201

unlocked and gone in, found Pantelaras dead, lost his head and bolted—and later remembered that as he'd been approaching the house, he'd seen a mysterious stranger coming away from it.'

Mr. Griffin jerked forward in his chair.

'How did you know all that?' he asked sharply. 'Whom have you been in communication with in Monte Carlo?'

'It's merely what the detective said your son-in-law was bound to start saying sooner or later,' Alistair answered.

It was dismaying that at that point Mrs. Griffin burst violently into tears.

Rose drew her breath in sharply. She leant towards Mrs. Griffin and looked as if she were about to speak. Then she drew back, folding her hands in her lap. Mr. Griffin gave his wife several little pats on the shoulder.

Through her tears, and drumming on the arms of her chair with her clenched fists, Mrs. Griffin cried out, 'He did see him—he did! Marie believes him and I believe Marie!'

Alistair felt moved and wanted to say something comforting and reassuring, and perhaps would have done so if he had not caught Rose's eye and seen a wary look of warning in it. He remembered then that the Griffins were still a long way from having given a satisfactory explanation of the anony-

202

mous letter or their search of the house.

He thought that Mr. Griffin noticed that interchange of looks. For the first time, Alistair felt positive hostility in the other man, but his voice, as he went on, was softer than before, smoother, more persuasive.

'It's been a great strain on us all, I'm afraid. We've felt—but I suppose that's clear—that we'd got to explore every avenue. And as my wife said earlier, you *were* there. And we knew that you'd come into Monte Carlo some time before your appointment with Pantelaras, because my wife saw you come into the Casino and leave again rather hurriedly when you saw us there—or later we thought that that must have been your reason for leaving so quickly. But I wish very much now we'd stayed on at Cap Martin and talked the whole affair over with you at the time, instead of leaving that night, as Marie advised. Of course you've realised by now that when you first saw Marie in the garden of the villa, she already knew of her father's death. Her husband had told her of it. But she wanted to save her mother all the distress she could, and urged me very strongly to take her away at once. If we'd stayed on, however, and talked frankly, as we have to-day, I doubt if we'd have built up any suspicion of you.'

In a low voice, Rose asked her first question, 'Why?'

Mr. Griffin looked unsure of what she meant.

'Why,' she repeated, 'have you given up your suspicion of us?'

He gave an abrupt laugh. 'Because, Mrs. Dirke, the behaviour of you and your husband, when we sent you that mysterious letter, and when you saw that coin on the Joy Wheel, and when you realised that I'd been searching your house, was just what it should have been if you were perfectly innocent. You were upset and angry, and in the one case went straight to the police, in one went straight and quite openly to your local expert, and in the third came straight to us, to ask us what we were up to. Incidentally, I hope this is a reasonably honest neighbourhood, because your house is remarkably easy to burgle.'

'But if you were searching our house for a collection of coins,' Rose said, 'you can't possibly have proved to yourself that it isn't there. It may be under a floorboard, or up a chimney, or buried in the garden.'

'True, but I was looking for something else besides a collection of coins,' he said, 'and, as it happens, I found it. I found evidence everywhere that you and your husband were just what you claimed to be, two people leading quite full and pleasant lives, in cheerful surroundings and with a variety of interests. That, incidentally, was the information about you given to us by the police here, when we went to see them on first arriving here. And in my view, it isn't among such people as I'm now convinced you really are, that murderers are to be found.'

'And that's the only reason why you're not suspicious of us any more?' Rose said.

'Good heavens, Mrs. Dirke, do you *want* me to go on suspecting you?'

'I was only wondering,' she said, 'if the truth might not be that since coming here you've found evidence that's made you suspect somebody else.'

She stood up.

Alistair was not sure that he was ready to leave yet. There were a few more questions in his mind that he would have liked to ask the Griffins. But in Rose's swift movement he recognised a decision to leave at once, and knew that he would either have to leave as well, or let her go without him.

As he stood up, he asked, 'Did your son-in-law describe the mysterious stranger?'

'He said he was a tall man, who wore a cap and a mackintosh and carried a bag,' Mr. Griffin answered. 'He said he noticed him mainly because of the mackintosh, which looked English, and in spite of the threat of rain that day, was rather heavy to be wearing on a summer day in Monte Carlo.'

'That's a very good description of a very mysterious stranger,' Alistair said, 'but not really helpful.'

He followed Rose to the door. As he went out, he heard Mrs. Griffin addressing her husband in a volley of excited whispers.

Driving back to Rollway, Alistair and Rose said very little to one another. As they started, he asked her why she had suddenly been in such a hurry to leave, but she answered only with an impatient little gesture, as if all that mattered now was to go home as fast as possible. He seldom drove fast, and all the way home he could feel her impatience.

It distracted him, because what he wanted at that moment was to think quietly. He wanted to think about what seemed to him the most important thing that had emerged during the interview, the difference between the two versions, which, it appeared, Nikolo Pantelaras had given his daughter and Henry Wallbank, of his intentions concerning the disposal of his collection. For in a way it made better sense that Pantelaras should have decided to give his collection away for nothing, than that he should have offered to sell it for far less than it was worth. But if that had been his real intention, the question of what had been behind his offer to the Purslem Collection remained as puzzling as ever.

They were nearly home when Rose asked him what he intended to do next.

'When we get home? Have a drink,' he said.

'Yes, but then?'

'Probably another.'

'Yes, but I mean about all this—about the Griffins—about everything.'

'What do you want me to do?' he asked. 'In there you suddenly seemed to know just what had to be done.'

She shook her head. 'I only wanted to get away. I couldn't stand it any more. I didn't know whether to be sorry for them and admire them for being ready to go to almost any lengths to help that girl, or to loathe them as a pair of very smooth liars.'

'They are rather smooth,' he said, 'and they work very well together. Perhaps when I've taken you home, I ought to go back to the police and tell them about that search.'

'Perhaps,' she said.

'Isn't it really the obvious thing to do? I'm strongly in favour of allowing the police to do their own jobs.'

'I suppose so. But what will you tell them?'

'That we want to be left in peace. That we want to have a chance to live our own lives!'

She turned her face to him with a sudden vivid smile. 'Tell them just that!'

'Well, it's what they're there for, isn't it? I *will* tell them just that.'

He meant it, when he said it, with a simple clarity of purpose. Yet he did not do it. It was not until much later that he again had contact with the police in Floxsted. For when he and Rose arrived home, Irene came running to meet them.

She was pale, with spots of bright colour in her cheeks.

'I've been to try to see Paul again and he isn't there,' she cried. 'The house is all shut up and I've knocked and I've called and nobody answered. Oh lord, I never thought it would be like this when I said I'd come here! I thought he'd be glad to see me. I thought we could make friends. But he hates me so much still, he's actually gone right away to avoid me.'

Rose, who had just got out of the car, stared at Irene unbelievingly. Then she burst into tears and went running into the house.

CHAPTER THIRTEEN

Alistair might have followed her in. Possibly that was what he ought to have done. Instead he decided to put the car away in the garage. Stubbornly, perversely, he saw this act as something that it was absolutely necessary for him to do at that moment.

As he drove the car into the garage, he was aware that Irene called something after him in a tone of protest, but he did not hear what it was. He put the car away, locked the garage and walked slowly back to the house. His movements were leaden. He felt as tired as he might have felt if he had just arrived at the end of a long journey.

Going into the sitting-room, he poured himself out a drink and sat down by the fireplace. As steadily as if there had been the flicker of flames there to hypnotise him, he stared at the empty hearth. He heard Irene come into the room, help herself to a drink and drop into a chair, but it did not seem important to notice her.

Overhead he could hear footsteps that went quickly backwards and forwards from corner to corner of the room above. He counted the number of steps in each direction. It was seventeen. Then, after a little while, the foot-steps stopped, but he went on counting up to seventeen and starting again at one, as if he could still hear them.

But he could not go on counting imaginary footsteps for ever. At some point he would have to admit that the thing had happened that he had been warding off all the summer. Rose had remorselessly given herself away to him. And now that it had happened, there could be no going back on it. The blind eye and the deaf ear were no longer defences against her. She had forced him to recognise her feelings, driven him to a point where he would have to make up his mind what it all meant to him. She had cornered him, trapped him.

Or was that all wrong? Was there some profound error in this view of the situation? Was there still a way out?

But as soon as he thought of that possi-bility, he dismissed it, for the truth seemed to be that now at last he did not want a way out. He did not want to go upstairs either, even though Rose, he thought, was probably wait-ing for him anxiously, and in her way in great need of him. Yet he felt no anger against her. In fact, in some ways, he felt more tenderness than he had honestly felt for a long time.

That, it seemed to him, was a rather

curious discovery. He sat thinking about it, nursing his glass between his hands, then presently he put it down untasted. Getting up, he walked out of the room. He let himself quietly out of the house and started walking along the road. He walked slowly, his head bent, his hands in his pockets.

There one of them suddenly encountered an unfamiliar object.

His fingers explored it and it took him a moment to identify it. It was Ted Boley's lucky piece, Mrs. Griffin's bracelet-charm, the prize of Nikolo Pantelaras's collection, the silver decadrachm of Syracuse, with the head of a beautiful woman on one side and a triumphal chariot on the other. He had forgotten that it was still in his possession.

Well, never mind, that was where it could remain for the present.

'Alistair . . .'

Swift, clicking footsteps had followed him along the road. A hand grabbed his elbow.

'Alistair, I don't know what you think you're doing,' Irene panted. 'If you're thinking of going to murder Paul, he isn't worth it. And anyway, he isn't there.'

'Murder?' Alistair said vaguely, wondering why that, of all words, should have been spoken just then.

'Your face,' Irene said. 'Darling, I was

simply terror-struck, sitting in there with you. Of course, even a moron like me's read somewhere or other that we've all got murder in us, but really! And just because . . . Well, I don't know why exactly. If you ask me, there's something a bit queer going on, and things aren't what they seem.'

'When did you acquire the habit of under-statement, Irene?' he asked. 'It strikes me as new.'

'Yes, that's what I think—I mean, something's actually *very* queer,' she said. 'I'm glad you think so. I was afraid you thought it was all just a straightforward triangular sort of thing, which wouldn't make sense.'

'Why wouldn't it make sense?' He was wishing, as he walked steadily ahead, that she would go back to the house, but with her arm linked in his, she kept trotting briskly at his side. 'It's been known to happen before.'

'Not with you and Rose!'

'Well, no.'

'That would destroy my last, my very last illusion. As it is, we can settle down quietly and think out what's really been happening.'

The idea of Irene settling down quietly in order, of all things, to think, moved in him a dim sense of amusement. Then he realised that she was tugging at his arm, trying to make him stop.

212

'Look, darling,' she said, 'let's go back. Do let's go back and do a little sensible thinking.'

'Presently,' he said.

'But Paul isn't there! It *is* Paul you're going to see, isn't it? He really isn't there. Don't you believe me?'

'I'm not sure,' he said. 'He might merely have stayed hidden till you'd gone.'

'Even when I shouted up at his window that if he didn't come out I'd go into his studio and smash every damn' thing I could find?'

He stood still at last and looked into her face. It was flushed and belligerent and, it dawned on him, a little frightened.

'You really did that, Irene?'

'Smash his things up? Of course not. But I did say I would,' she answered. 'And he'd have believed me, because once I—oh well, we needn't go into that. But if he'd been there, he'd have come running. So now let's go back and cheer Rose up, shall we? Do come, darling.'

There was an intensity in the appeal that surprised him. But he said, 'We're almost there and he may have come back by now.'

'But what are you going to say when you see him?'

And there, of course, she had him, because he had not the faintest idea, so he walked on

213

again, a little too fast for Irene, on her high heels. But she came stubbornly trotting after him, damning him, Paul, all men and the country road.

When he reached the lodge, he found it, as Irene had told him, all shut up, with the upper as well as the lower windows carefully closed, and when he knocked, first at the front door, then at the back, he heard no sound whatever inside the little house.

Irene, asking him repeatedly if she hadn't told him so, had followed him round the house, and then followed him to the studio in the garden.

This he found unlocked, but a glance showed him that Paul was not there. There were many pieces of Paul's work on the shelves round the walls, and on a turntable on a wooden pedestal in the centre of the room was something wrapped in a damp cloth, which suggested that Paul must be intending to return in the near future. But as Alistair closed the door again, he had to agree that it looked as if Paul had suddenly gone away.

Alistair did not know yet what that might mean to him, because he did not know yet precisely why he had felt that first, before doing anything else, he must make sure whether or not it was true that Paul had gone away. But he was aware, in finding Paul

214

gone, of a sense of frustration. There were things it would have been pleasant, very pleasant to do, if he had found him.

That being so, it would shortly, no doubt, be a great relief to Alistair that Paul had gone away in time, but for the moment he was left in a tense, bewildered state of suspended excitement, unable to see anything or to think clearly.

It was for this reason that he quite failed, until many hours later, to recognise the strangeness of the unlocked studio.

That came to him all of a sudden in the early morning. He had lain awake all night, as Rose also, he believed, had lain awake. Yet they had still scarcely spoken to one another since Rose had burst into tears at the news that Paul had gone away. When Alistair and Irene had arrived back at the house, they had found Rose frying chops, laying the table and very rapidly and ostentatiously doing several other things at the same time, with a don't-dare-to-interrupt-me air about her. When the meal was ready and they had sat down at the table, she had given Alistair one swift, haunted look, then she had started talking to Irene about the fête, and Irene, as if she thought she were helping, had started one of her monologues about herself, which, so it had seemed, she was prepared to keep up for the rest of the evening.

It had driven Alistair, as soon as the meal was over, to his room, where he had got out some notes that he had not looked at since he and Rose had gone away for their holiday, and had tried to do some work. At about one in the morning he had crept quietly upstairs to bed. Rose had lain very still and kept her eyes shut and he had let her believe that he had accepted her pretence of sleep.

It was at about four o'clock that the thought about Paul's studio suddenly struck him. The thought was simply that Paul, who was normally very careless of his possessions, but was fantastically sensitive about anyone seeing his work uninvited, would never have gone away, leaving his house carefully locked up and his studio unlocked.

If the studio had been locked and the house unlocked, there would have been nothing surprising about it. But as it was, there was something out of joint in the situation. Something was strange. Something was wrong.

Not that Alistair yet had any clear suspicion of what it was. It was startling to him later to realise how little suspicion he had had, blinded as he had been by his conviction that Paul had gone away to escape the pain of Rose's nearness, or even, for this possibility had seemed vivid and convincing for a part of

216

that everlasting night, a temptation that had scared him by being too freely offered. The first daylight and the birds trying out their early morning notes, then joining in their exuberant dawn chorus, had driven that bitter thought of the darkness away, but the puzzle of the unlocked studio had remained as a nagging drag at Alistair's imagination, so that the last hope of an hour or two of sleep vanished. At about seven o'clock, before Rose had stirred, he got up, dressed, went softly downstairs and out into the cool, fresh morning.

He went back to the lodge, but to-day, instead of knocking at either door of the house, since there was no certainty that Paul, even if he had returned, would be awake at seven o'clock, Alistair went straight to the studio. Its door was still unlocked. Inside, everything was as it had been the day before, except that the damp cloth, wrapped around the unfinished work on the turntable, had dried in the heat of the sultry night. Returning to the house, he saw that the windows, including that of Paul's bedroom, were still closed.

Alistair then did something that he might have done the day before if he had not had Irene with him, tugging at his arm, urging him to come away. He walked all round the

217

house, looking in at the windows.

They were narrow, pointed, Gothic windows with leaded panes. Through the kitchen window he could see the whole of the kitchen, and see that it was empty and tidy. But through the window in the front of the house, one curtain of which was partially drawn, as if to keep out yesterday's too bright sunshine, he could by no means see the whole of the sitting-room. He could see, however, that the high-backed sofa, which normally stood directly under the window, had been pulled away from the wall and now stood senselessly in the middle of the room.

That seemed a curious piece of disorder, for the sofa had not been pulled close to a light, or to a table, or to a position that appeared to have anything else to recommend it. Alistair considered it for a minute or two, then made up his mind what to do next.

Paul's house was cleaned for him by Mrs. Bycraft, a woman who lived in a cottage near to the Maybush. The day being Sunday, it was not to be expected that she would be coming to work that morning, but she was probably to be found at home. Alistair, therefore, set off to the village, went to the Bycrafts' cottage, knocked, and when the door was opened by Mrs. Bycraft, a solid, cheerful, untidy woman, with her grey hair in curlers, he asked her if she knew anything about Mr. Eckleston's sudden departure, or when he was likely to return.

She said that she knew nothing whatever about any intention of Mr. Eckleston's to go away for the week-end. She also said a great deal else on a number of quite unrelated subjects. It took a determined repetition of certain questions to bring her back to Paul. She said then that she had seen him the morning before, and that it was true that he had said something vaguely about going abroad somewhere some time, but she was sure he hadn't meant right away, and that he wasn't one to go off without telling her, because he liked her to go in and water his plants and all that. It was a bit queer, she thought, if he had gone away like that, and maybe she ought to go over and see if everything was all right. There was the milk, for instance. Had he thought to stop it? If not, you wouldn't want it standing in the hot sun all day. And if the paper lay there on the doorstep from morning till night, it told everyone there was no one at home, didn't it? But as Mrs. Bycraft said all this, she kept glancing towards the stove, where the kettle was just coming to the boil and the teapot was keeping warm, and when Alistair asked her if she had a key to Mr. Eckleston's house, she said rather eagerly that she had, and that, knowing Professor Dirke, she was sure it would be all right to let him have it, just to make sure that Mr. Eckleston hadn't been taken ill, or anything.

Pocketing the key, promising to bring it back almost immediately, Alistair returned to the lodge, unlocked the front door and pushed it open.

There had been a time, standing on the doorstep of a villa in Monte Carlo, ringing a bell that no one had answered, when Alistair's imagination, leaping ahead, had warned him of the robbery and murder that had happened inside the silent house. He had dismissed that warning. If Marie Robinet had not arrived when she did, he would have rung the bell perhaps once more, or twice, then gone away.

This time he had not ignored the premonition, intuition, or whatever it was, that had come to him in the early hours of that morning. Acting, as it had, on the already half-realised sense of calamity that had been with him ever since the day before, when Irene had cried out that Paul had gone and Rose had burst into betraying tears, this experience had a little prepared Alistair for what he would find here on the high-backed sofa, the sofa which had so plainly been moved so that what lay upon it could not be

220

seen from the window. Also, to some extent, it lessened the shock and gave him a moment of curious calm in which to take a firm hold on his feelings. But also, for a minute or two, it deceived him.

For what he had feared had been Paul's suicide, and here in the room with his dead body was the gun that could have dropped from his hand. And it seemed certain, thinking of the unlocked studio, and adding one incident to another, from the time when Paul and he had walked back to this house and Paul had told him that he had decided, after all, to go away, that the fear of Paul's suicide was the horror that had hung on Rose's mind and caused her breakdown and her sleepless night.

But after that first minute, Alistair recognised that it was murder that had happened here. For if Paul had wanted to make sure that he would die in private, he could have gone upstairs to his bedroom, or he could simply have drawn the curtains. There would have been no need for him to move the sofa to that odd position in the middle of the room to provide a screen between his dead body and the windows. And in no circumstances would he have thought of huddling himself into that contorted position on the sofa, when he could have sat in a chair or lain on a bed.

Thinking this out, Alistair had not moved from the doorway. There was a terrible warmth in the room. All the heat of the last few days seemed to have been locked up inside it. There was a heavy scent of roses, tinged with decay and over-sweet.

Behind him lay the park of Purslem Manor, the grass already greener for yesterday's rain, the smooth slopes bright and quiet in the early sunlight. He felt an intense reluctance to shut this out, and to step into the small shadowed room, to be alone with Paul, towards whom, in the sense that he himself was a part, perhaps the most important part, of Paul's tragedy, he had felt a horrified sense of guilt.

But if this was murder, these were not feelings which should be allowed to confuse the issue. And the truth must be that Paul had been shot when he was sitting on the sofa, in front of the window, talking to his murderer. The murderer had then at once realised that anyone coming to the house could see the body, and had started to draw the curtains. But then he had realised that if anyone in the park were to see this happen, that moment would later be known as the time when the murder had been committed. So leaving the curtains as they were, he had moved Paul's body, so that instead of sitting sprawled on the sofa, as it must have been after the shooting, it lay almost doubled up along the seat. Then the murderer had somehow pulled the sofa, with its heavy burden on it, away from the window to the middle of the room.

Oh yes, it was murder and there were things to be done immediately.

First, the police must be sent for. Alistair stepped into the room, closing the door softly, as if the sound of it could disturb Paul's quiet, then went to the telephone. It was the local police station that he rang up and he spoke to Sergeant Wragg. Then he put the telephone down again and took another long look round the room.

It was only then that he saw what had been out of sight while he stood in the doorway. Lying on the tiled hearth, broken into fragments, was the terra-cotta figure of Nikolo Pantelaras.

That was the moment when for the first time Alistair began to connect Paul Eckleston with what had happened in Monte Carlo. Until then, it had never once occurred to him to make that connection. Not even a shadow of a suspicion of it had crossed his mind. Seeing Paul dead, and seeing, in the false calm of those first moments, the evidence that pointed to murder, Alistair's suspicions had leapt wildly towards Irene. With a prick-

223

ling up his spine at the memory, he had remembered the dragging hand on his elbow and the persuasive voice that had tried so hard to make him go home to Rose.

But what interest could Irene have in Nikolo Pantelaras? And if she had hurled that figure down on to the hearth, not because it was of Pantelaras, but simply in a spasm of destructive rage against Paul and all his works, would she ever have said anything afterwards of her shouted threat at Paul, that she would go into his studio and smash up all that she found there? Surely not even Irene would go as far as that in unnecessary frankness.

The little clay head, snapped clean off the body, but itself unbroken, lay on the hearth, with the grey mask-like face, topped by the piebald hair, looking up at Alistair.

Sharply he recalled Henry's exclamation that he thought Paul only did this sort of thing from the life, and Paul's swift reply that he did not do much of this sort of thing at all. Then Paul had gone on to say that after the talk about Pantelaras in the Dirkes' garden, he had started thinking about him. Had that been the truth? Had this figure been made from Paul's memory of a man not seen for several years, or from one seen recently?

What that question might have led to Alistair never learnt, for that was when he heard Rose's scream in the doorway.

He turned round.

She was standing there, leaning weakly against the doorpost, her eyes on Paul, her hands over her mouth to choke back a second scream. Alistair was not sure that she had seen him.

But when he reached her, she came straight into his arms and hid her face against him. She was trembling from head to foot. He held her closely, then gently tried to turn her so that her back was towards the room.

He meant to take her out into the garden, to close the door, to stay out there until the police came. But she resisted him. She clung to him, but he could not make her move. Then, with a shudder, she lifted her head and looked straight at Paul. As she did so, the empty look of shock passed out of her eyes and they filled with pity.

Her voice came in a whisper. 'It's the best thing, isn't it?'

He looked at her in astonishment. 'The *best* thing. . . ?'

'Better than . . .' She stopped. She withdrew her wide-eyed gaze from the dead man's face and let it dwell on Alistair's. 'Of course, you don't know why he did it. It wasn't because of me. He was in love with me in his way, but he wouldn't have killed himself because of it.'

'He didn't kill himself,' Alistair said. 'He was murdered.'

She looked so uncomprehending that he told her, in a few words, why Paul's death could not have been suicide.

When he stopped, she gave a little nod, as if something that had puzzled her were now quite clear.

'So there was someone else who knew all the time,' she said.

'Knew what?' Alistair asked.

'About Pantelaras. That it was Paul.'

She started to turn away from him, but he grabbed her shoulders and jerked her back to face him.

'You're telling me that it was Paul who murdered Pantelaras?'

'Of course,' she said.

'You're telling me Paul came to Monte Carlo, murdered Pantelaras and stole his coins?'

He saw her eyes fill with tears. 'Of course, of course! It's been so plain all along. But you never listened to me when I started trying to tell you. It was all in that letter.'

This time, as she started to move away from him, he let her go.

What she had said struck him as complete

226

nonsense, but then his eye fell on the severed terra-cotta head lying on the hearth, and his mind went back to the question that he had started to ask himself when he heard Rose scream.

'Let's get out of here,' he said. 'Let's get outside and try to talk. We haven't got long. The police will be here at any minute.'

'All right.' With her handkerchief to her eyes, mopping at the tears that were brimming over, she took a couple of unsteady steps towards the doorway.

But it happened that it was the nearest doorway towards which she had instinctively moved, and that was not the door by which she had come in, but the door into the kitchen. Realising her mistake, she stood still.

Then she said sharply, 'Look!'

He went to her side. He looked where she was pointing.

The kitchen was a very small one, which at the time the house was built had probably been intended merely as a scullery, while the present sitting-room would have been the family kitchen for the lodge-keeper and his wife. This little kitchen, with its modern fittings, was very neat and clean. There were no unwashed dishes in the sink, no cooking-pots on the stove. But clearly printed on the pale grey linoleum was a pattern of muddy footmarks. Starting at the back door, they went to the sink, then from the sink to the door of the sitting-room. If they continued beyond that, they were invisible on the carpet. They had been made by a pair of shoes with rubber soles, the pattern of which, with a small diamond-shaped trade-mark in the centre, was plainly outlined in dried mud on the clean floor.

'I think they're Paul's,' Alistair said.

Rose glanced towards the sofa. 'Yes—then I suppose they aren't important. I thought for a moment . . .'

'But I think they *are* important—very,' Alistair said. 'But let's get outside. I want you to tell me about the letter before the police come.'

She nodded and let him guide her towards the other door and out into the garden.

The grass was wet with dew, too wet to sit on. They went down the path to the garden gate and leant their elbows on it.

'You mean that letter Paul wrote to you when we were at Cap Martin?' Alistair said.

'Yes—but why are those footsteps important if they're only Paul's?'

Impatiently he answered, 'Because it didn't rain until the middle of the afternoon. If there's any doubt about the time he was murdered, if the police can't get it from the

228

state of the body, those footsteps at least mean that Paul wasn't killed until after the storm broke. He must have been out in the studio when the rain started and got the mud on to his shoes as he came back to the house. Then I suppose he went to the sink, washed his hands there, and then went into the sitting-room. And that may mean he was expecting a visit from his murderer. . . . But about the letter, Rose.'

She had screwed up her eyes, as if she found the sunshine too bright, or else were trying to concentrate on some baffling problem.

'But I don't see . . .'

'The letter.'

'Yes. You ought to have read it,' she said, 'but you wouldn't, because you thought it was a love-letter. And it—it was, in a way. But also it said that Paul knew when Pantelaras was going to get his coins out of the bank, and felt inclined to turn up and steal them. Of course I—I thought that was a joke. I tried to think the whole letter was a joke. And so, when I answered, on a card that I got at the same time as the one we sent to Henry, I simply said we were having a lovely holiday, and took no notice of anything he'd said. And I let you see me post the card, because I was so furious with you about—about everything.'

'Have you still got the letter?' Alistair asked.

'No.'

'But all this time you've been believing it was Paul who'd murdered Pantelaras?'

'*Believing* it—no,' she said. 'Not really. Not all the time. Only sometimes, when he said or did certain things. And then I'd decide it couldn't be true. You ought to know how one can do that. I believed it last night, though. When Irene said he'd gone, I thought he must have got frightened by the Griffins, coming here, and decided to go off abroad with the coins.'

Alistair caught his breath. Then speaking carefully, feeling that it needed a great effort to stick to the subject, he said, 'And was that your whole reason for thinking that Paul was a murderer—just that letter and that joke? Because if it was, you've been living in an unnecessary nightmare. The last thing he'd have done, if he'd really intended to commit a crime, was to write and tell you that he was thinking of committing it.'

She turned her head towards him. 'You didn't see that letter.'

'No.'

'He—he said some extraordinary things in it about money. He thought that it was because he hadn't much money that Irene had left him, and he seemed to think that if he had more than he had, I—I might have left you.'

'Wait—we can settle this,' Alistair said. 'We can find out quite simply whether or not Paul went to Monte Carlo. Wait here a moment.'

He turned and went back to the house.

As he had so often seen it in the past, the flap of the bureau in the sitting-room was open and covered with an untidy litter of papers. He fumbled hurriedly through them and through the pigeon-holes, which were jammed with old letters. Almost at once he found what he was looking for, the slim book, covered in dark blue, which was in one of the pigeon-holes, between a couple of receipted bills. He opened it, absolutely certain that in a moment he would be able to prove to Rose that her suspicions of Paul were utterly groundless.

He stared. It seemed impossible. But there, on one of the pink pages in Paul's passport, among a number of other stamps, were the stamps that had been made on his entering and leaving France on the day before and the day following the murder of Nikolo Pantelaras.

So Rose had been right. Paul was the

mysterious stranger in the raincoat, seen by Robinet near the villa. Paul had stolen the collection of coins. Paul was the murderer of Pantelaras.

And that made the motive for Paul's murder perfectly clear.

With the passport still in his hand, Alistair turned to the door, as voices outside told him that the police had arrived.

CHAPTER FOURTEEN

More than anything else during the time that followed, Alistair wanted to be alone with Rose. After a short while he was able to go to her in the garden, where she had remained when the men who had arrived from Floxsted streamed into the little, suffocating room. He was able to whisper to her that her guess had been right, that the evidence against Paul was there in his passport. But to talk to her as he wanted to talk was impossible and was likely to remain so, he saw, for several hours.

There were people all round them and a constant coming and going of men in and out of uniform. There were questions to be answered. For the moment these were only about how he had happened to discover the murder, but he knew that there would soon be many other questions to come.

At the request of the police, he and Rose stayed in the garden and were glad not to have to remain in the house. But the garden would have been a less uncomfortable place to stay, if it had been better concealed from the road. The police had closed the lodge gates and were allowing no one through them, but as the news of the murder spread through the village, a crowd collected out-side, with noses glued to the spaces in the wrought iron. Paul's garden seemed very naked of shelter.

The man in charge of the police was tall and heavily built with an irritable, crumpled, pug-dog face, a face which Alistair thought the man himself might be persuaded was a bulldog face, though in fact its features were too insignificant and without the bulldog's statuesque melancholy. But the slightly bulg-ing eyes on either side of the small, crushed-looking nose were sharp and intelligent, and the man did not snap or yap, but for the most part, hands in pockets and heavy shoulders slack, remained rather morosely silent.

He was presently called to the gate by the constable on guard there, as some excitement broke out in the crowd in the road. Someone was calling out and trying to push a way through. Alistair could not hear what was said, but a minute or two later the gates were opened a little way and Mrs. Bycraft, with an old mackintosh on over an apron and her hair still in curlers, came bursting through.

She came running straight to Rose and Ali-stair.

'There now, Mr. Dirke, you were right, weren't you, there was something wrong!' she cried. 'I said so myself, I said, he wouldn't have gone away without letting me know, I said. But oh, Mrs. Dirke, what a thing to happen, what a terrible thing! Poor Mr. Eckleston, he was always so kind, I always said so, he's so kind and thoughtful, I said, he ought to be married, he'd make some woman a wonderful husband, I said, always carrying the coals in himself and not criticising.'

She was crying a little, mopping at her eyes and self-consciously patting her curlers.

'I heard the news down in the village,' she went on, 'and I come right off, just popped my mac on and never gave a thought to my hair. Being Sunday, me and Mr. Bycraft was taking it easy, but I come out at once when I heard the news. Maybe there's something I can do, I said to Mr. Bycraft, if it's only to make a pot of tea for somebody.'

'Tea!' Alistair exclaimed. It was the first time since he had let himself into the house that the thought had occurred to him that he had not had any breakfast. 'That's a wonderful idea, Mrs. Bycraft. Oh, but I'm afraid they won't let you into the kitchen. And that reminds me—' He thought this might be the last opportunity for some time to come to ask her what seemed to him a very important question. 'Do you happen to remember when you last cleaned the kitchen floor?'

He saw the suspicion come instantly into her mind that, unlike Paul, he was one who criticised, and he wished that he had phrased the question differently.

'Last thing,' she answered. 'I always do it last thing on a Saturday, so's to leave it nice for the weekend. And I scrubbed it good and proper, like I always do.'

'Ah, I thought it looked very clean,' he said, 'very clean indeed. Except for the footprints. That's why they showed up so plainly, of course—because the floor was so clean.'

'Footprints?' she said and her tearful eyes brightened with interest. But a constable came then to take her to talk to the pug-faced man.

As she went away, Rose remarked, 'And now here's Henry.'

Alistair turned.

Henry was trotting down the avenue from the manor-house. He was puffing and stumbling and red with agitation, holding his spectacles on with one hand and waving the other to attract their attention.

'What's all this, eh?' he demanded as he reached the garden gate and thrust his way through it. 'Whatever's happened? Could see from our windows something was wrong. Saw crowds—not supposed to come in the park on a Sunday morning—everyone knows

236

that. Didn't see it was police till I got close. Something to do with Paul, eh? Something wrong?'

'Very wrong,' Alistair answered.

He meant to go on, after giving Henry a moment to brace himself to hear the news. But before he could do so, Rose, leaning towards Henry, spoke into his ear in a fierce undertone. 'It's murder, Henry. Paul's been murdered.'

Henry took a step backwards. He winced as if she had hit him. Then he seemed to collect his wits, looked at her steadily and said thoughtfully, 'You're not joking. No, I can see that. Serious, both of you. That's even worse than I thought. Don't know what I did think, though. Saw police, knew it meant trouble, but never thought . . .'

His bald head was beaded with sweat. He pulled a handkerchief out of his pocket and wiped it over his face and forehead.

Rose's tone had taken Alistair by surprise, though he understood how her mind was working. Paul had been murdered for the sake of the coins that he had stolen from Nikolo Pantelaras. Henry was interested in coins. Adding those two facts together made a very simple little piece of mental arithmetic. But it seemed necessary to Alistair to apologise to Henry for it, because Henry was looking old and sick and flustered.

'I'm sorry we had to give you such a shock, Henry,' Alistair said.

Henry's glance darted towards him. It was an acute glance, clear and understanding. For an instant it was like the glance that he had cast at the coin, the silver decadrachm, the day before. Alistair found himself wondering if Henry had put two and two together as quickly as Rose.

But Henry's mumbled answer about its being quite all right and how frightful it was, was as confused as ever, until, turning his head and seeing the pug-faced man in the doorway, he said, 'That's Inspector Lack. That's good. Good man. Just wait for me a moment, will you? Got an idea.'

He shambled off before Alistair could assure him that there appeared to be nothing else they could do but wait for him.

But Henry's idea turned out to be, in Alistair's view, an extremely good one. Coming back in a few minutes' time, having been inside the house with the inspector and re-emerged paler, yet somehow steadier, for the experience, Henry took each of them by the arm and said, 'Just fixed it up with Lack. We'll go over to our house. Better than standing around here being stared at. Mrs. Bycraft's coming too. Lack can get hold of any of us any time he wants. And Agnes can make us some coffee. Give you some breakfast too, if you haven't had any.'

The thought of food did not seem to Alistair particularly attractive, but the promise of coffee seemed wonderful. He started willingly towards the gate, then realised that Rose had pulled away from Henry's grasp.

'What about Irene?' she said.

'Yes indeed, Irene,' Alistair said, wondering how he could have forgotten her. 'We ought to get hold of her. She doesn't even know about this yet.'

'Wait!' Henry said, and rushed off to find his friend Lack again.

'Oh dear, we oughtn't to have let this happen,' Rose said in distress. 'He'll tell them all about Irene and Paul, and heaven knows what that'll make them think about her. Perhaps they won't even let us go to her, and we might have helped to cushion the shock for her a little.'

'Will she care, then?' Alistair asked, curious to see what she thought.

'Of course she'll care. Wouldn't anyone?' Rose said.

'But Irene particularly?'

'I think so.'

'Then did she come here really to make it up with him?'

'To make peace with him, anyway.'

He recognised the difference between the two statements, but was not yet convinced that either was true.

Seeing the doubt on his face, Rose said, 'I think she's always had Paul on her conscience. I think she believed she did him a great deal of harm. And now that she's become so successful, she wanted more than ever to be able to feel that he didn't hate her. In a way, I suppose you can call it a selfish way to feel. What she wanted was an easy and painless absolution. On the other hand, it's come about at least partly because she's forgiven him the harm he did her.'

'And did he hate her?' he asked.

'I'm afraid he did.' Then, as Henry and the pug-faced man approached them together, she said, 'Yes, Henry's managed to do his worst for her.'

Henry himself seemed to have realised this. He looked downcast and nervous. The inspector, in his sullen-seeming way, told Rose and Alistair that the information concerning Miss Byrd's relationship with the dead man was extremely interesting, and that a car had been despatched to fetch her. Rose and Alistair said that in that case they would wait here for her, but were then told by Lack that as a matter of fact the sergeant in charge

240

might exercise his discretion and take her to Floxsted, to protect her from the staring of the crowd here. Alistair went on arguing about it for a little, but then agreed to be sent off with Rose, Mrs. Bycraft and Henry, to the Wallbanks' house.

As they started across the park, Henry apologised unhappily. 'Damn' silly of me, never thought of the implications. Was thinking only the poor girl ought to be told the news without delay. She's a tough little thing, though. Won't go to pieces, eh? And after all, it's not as if he was actually her husband any more.'

Alistair nudged him sharply, giving a warning nod at Mrs. Bycraft.

'Oh, yes, quite, quite,' Henry muttered.

After that it was a silent walk towards the house in the grove of trees.

On their right, as they went, the windows of the great house glittered with reflections of the early sunlight. The angle of the light and some faint blue haziness in the air made the sprawling building look farther away than it really was, just as, at evening, with the sun setting behind it, it seemed to overshadow the whole park.

There was no sign of Agnes as they approached the Wallbanks' house. Even when Henry opened the door and called out to her, there was at first no sign of her. But when they went into the sitting-room they found her down on her hands and knees in a corner, her face fiercely set, her teeth gritted, as she polished the linoleum that showed round the edges of the worn carpet.

She seemed unwilling to stop polishing and get up, even when Henry, his voice full of tender consideration, as if he dreaded the effect that the information might have on her nerves, told her the reason for the crowd by the lodge-gates. As she listened to him, she frowned, her features twitched and her lips moved in a few inaudible exclamations, but she went on looking threateningly at the linoleum which she had not yet had a chance to assault. But in the end some slow-acting sense of propriety made her give a sigh, jam the lid back on to the tin of floor polish and stand up.

'If I said I'd told you so, that wouldn't be true, would it?' she said. 'I never did. I might have, but I didn't. I keep things like that to myself.'

Her voice was thin and quivering with an inexplicable self-righteousness. It was not one of Agnes's good days.

'Yes, dear,' Henry said. 'Now I've promised these people coffee. And some breakfast too, if they want it. We can do that, can't

242

we?'

'What d'you mean, we can do it? Of course we can do it,' she said. 'Do you think you can't rely on me to have coffee in my store cupboard? Do you think I may have forgotten to buy the eggs and bacon?'

'No, dear, I only meant—'

'You don't know what you meant, any more than I do half the time. You just talk for the sake of talking, as most people do. If some of them listened more, they'd know more. You can learn a lot by listening and thinking.' She looked sharply at Alistair. 'I suppose they suspect Miss Byrd.'

He was not prepared for the abrupt question. Before he could answer, Agnes swept on, 'The wife—they always suspect the wife. Stands to reason. Who else has the motive?'

A swift intake of breath from Mrs. Bycraft, as she stood in the doorway, patting her curlers, told Alistair that these words would be all round the village in no time at all, if he could not correct them.

He explained, 'She's his divorced wife—divorced several years ago. I can't imagine any motive she could have for murdering him.'

'I didn't say *I* suspected her, did I?' Agnes said. 'But that's what the police will think.

243

Sure to. All the same, who else could have any motive for murdering Paul? A very harmless sort of man, I always thought.'

'Yes,' Henry said, 'that's what I've been wracking my brains about ever since I got over there. Why? Can't seem to think clearly, though. Been awake most of the night, thinking about those Griffins and that coin. But this can't have anything to do with that, can it? But I can't think of any other reason—really can't. Unless, of course, Miss Byrd . . . No, I don't believe that. Charming girl.'

'I'm afraid it did have something to do with the coins,' Alistair said. 'There's evidence—'

But as if this possibility had no interest for her whatever, Agnes chose that moment to dart out of the room and start clattering cooking-pots in the kitchen.

Mrs. Bycraft gave Rose a significant glance. It expressed her view of people who polished floors on Sunday mornings, instead of, like herself and Mr. Bycraft, taking it easy. Then she advanced farther into the room and looked pointedly around for a place to sit down. It made Henry apologise and wave them all vaguely to chairs. Agnes, he said, would have breakfast ready in a jiffy. Trying to straighten his spectacles, he gave Alistair a wondering stare.

'You didn't actually say that, did you?' he said. 'I mean, that it's got something to do with the coins. Doesn't make sense, of course. Couldn't have been what you said. It's just that it's been on my mind so much, I keep hearing that sort of thing.'

'But it does make sense of a sort,' Alistair said.

He and Rose sat down side by side on the hard couch which jutted out at right angles from the wall beside the empty fireplace. Mrs. Bycraft chose an upright chair and sat down genteelly on the edge of it, wrapping her waterproof around her to conceal as much as possible of her apron. Henry hovered in the doorway, with an uneasy eye, as always, on Agnes's activities, while he puzzled over Alistair's answer.

'Don't understand you,' he said.

But something had just occurred to Alistair which was so important that he could not imagine why he had not thought of it before. Instead of answering, he went on thinking about it, while Henry fidgeted and gave a prompting little cough, and Mrs. Bycraft slid a hand rather furtively into a pocket of her coat and brought out a packet of Woodbines.

'Mind if I have a smoke, Mr. Wallbank?' she asked.

Henry started, told her to go ahead and

245

looked helplessly around for matches. Alistair found some in his pocket.

'Mrs. Bycraft, you always worked for Mr. Eckleston on a Saturday morning, didn't you?' he said, as he lit her cigarette.

She drew some smoke in thankfully and settled herself more comfortably on her chair.

'Yes, Mr. Dirke, Mondays, Wednesdays and Saturdays,' she said. 'I been doing that for three years now and I'll miss it, it was a nice little job, it just suited me. He let me go at it my own way, and never interfered, and he always brought the coals in himself, and never criticised. If there's a thing that puts me off at once, it's being interfered with when I'm working, but Mr. Eckleston never interfered—'

'Yes, Mrs. Bycraft, but you'd see him some time during the morning, I suppose,' Alistair interrupted. 'He didn't keep out of your way completely.'

'Well, naturally I'd see him, Mr. Dirke,' she said. 'I always made him a cup of tea middle of the morning, when I made one for myself, and took it to him out in the studio, or wherever he was. He always liked a cup of tea middle of the morning.'

'And did you see him as usual last Saturday morning?' Alistair asked. 'I don't mean yesterday, I mean a week ago.'

'A week ago? Why, that's the time you weren't well, wasn't it, Mr. Wallbank, and I came and helped out here?' she said. 'Yes, that's right, that was a week ago yesterday. Mr. Eckleston sent me a note down Wednesday evening, saying Mr. Wallbank wasn't well and Mrs. Wallbank wasn't too grand either, and would I oblige him by going over to help them, instead of coming to him? And that was just like him, Mr. Dirke, kind and thoughtful. Well, I couldn't come here Thursday or Friday, because Thursdays I go to the vicarage, and Fridays I visit my sister in Floxsted and take the little boy out and generally buy my meat too, so I don't like to change it around. But Saturday I came here, didn't I, Mr. Wallbank, and did the scrubbing and the downstairs windows for Mrs. Wallbank, and cleaned the kitchen stove? I'd have done more, only not the upstairs windows, because heights make me dizzy, but Mrs. Wallbank said that was all she wanted, so I went home and me and Mr. Bycraft went to the pictures.'

'So you didn't see Mr. Eckleston between Wednesday morning and the following Monday morning?' Alistair said.

'No, that's right, I didn't,' Mrs. Bycraft answered.

'Are you quite sure of that?'

'Look here, Alistair,' Henry exploded, 'what is all this?'

Alistair raised a warning eyebrow at him. 'Are you quite sure, Mrs. Bycraft?'

'Well, of course I'm sure, Mr. Dirke,' she said. 'I'd no reason to come around here over the week-end, had I? And Thursdays, you see, I go to the vicarage, and Fridays—'

'Yes, to your sister in Floxsted.' Alistair turned to Rose. She nodded.

'There's no way out,' she said. 'It *was* Paul. I've been going over and over it in my mind for days.'

Agnes appeared suddenly in the doorway.

'What was Paul?' she asked.

Alistair wished that she had stayed in the kitchen. He did not like the over-brightness of her eyes, or the excited tremor in her voice.

He answered reluctantly. 'There's some evidence that it may have been Paul who murdered Pantelaras. No—wait! That isn't as wild as it sounds. Paul did go to France on the Thursday, the day before the murder, and he left it on Saturday, the day after. The stamps are there in his passport. And now it's plain that he went more or less secretly. He didn't tell Mrs. Bycraft anything about going away, and he didn't tell either of you, did he? And somehow he knew that Pantelaras normally kept his collection in the bank, but that he would have it in his house on the Friday.'

'How did he know that?' Henry asked. 'Oh—good God! Why, I told him *that* myself. I remember. He asked me about it.'

There was a silence. Mrs. Bycraft merely looked confused at this talk of another murder. Henry looked incredulous. Only Agnes seemed to have taken in what Alistair had said.

'You mean it was Paul who stole the coins?' The dangerous, excitable tremor was still in her voice.

Rose replied, 'Stole the coins and the gun that was missing from the villa—the gun someone used to kill him yesterday. Yes, it was Paul. He told me . . .' She stopped. She pressed her hands together, as if that gesture would hold back the words.

'And he had the coins here all the time!' Agnes said. 'I knew he'd gone away, of course—I could have told you that. And he had the coins here, right under Henry's nose. And that's why someone killed him—to get the coins!'

To Alistair's horror, she began to giggle.

'To get the coins!' she cried. 'And who could that be but Henry? Who else would care enough about a lot of old coins? Who else will the police ever dream of suspecting,

249

once they've thought of Henry?'

Her voice had risen higher and higher. She ended in a wild laugh, then started to scream.

CHAPTER FIFTEEN

Mrs. Bycraft got up and took a couple of steps in Agnes's direction. Her face showed her intention. But the threat of it was enough and she had no need to carry it out. Between one scream and the next, Agnes seemed to lose her voice. Turning to Henry, she flung her arms round his neck and hid her face on his shoulder.

In a distressed voice, Henry murmured, 'I believe the kettle's boiling.'

'That's all right, I'll see to it,' Mrs. Bycraft said and went out to the kitchen.

Henry patted Agnes's shoulder and made vague, clucking noises. But his eyes were not vague.

'Must try to get this straight,' he said. 'Can't say I really follow you, though. First, Paul murders Pantelaras—that the idea? Leaves here on the quiet on Thursday, first arranging things so that Mrs. Bycraft won't go to him on the Saturday and find out he's away—oh, but how did he know I was going to be ill? How did he know Agnes was going to ask him on the Wednesday if we could borrow Mrs. Bycraft?'

'I don't suppose he did,' Alistair said. 'But

if you hadn't done it, he'd have thought of some other way of keeping her away.'

Agnes raised her head. 'I didn't ask if I could borrow Mrs. Bycraft. I'd never have dreamt of doing such a thing. It would have been most impertinent. It was Paul who persuaded me—pressed it on me, as a matter of fact. I wasn't even sure I wanted her, because you know what these women are like—a lick and a promise, sloshing a lot of water around and using up all your soap, and you have to do all the work over again after they've gone. I believe I did do everything she touched over again next day. She's a thoroughly sloppy worker.'

'Sh, dear,' Henry said with an uneasy glance towards the kitchen. 'Well, all right, then. Paul gets rid of Mrs. Bycraft, goes to Monte Carlo. How? Flies, I suppose.'

'No, train,' Alistair said. 'There are records of people who fly. But in the summer holiday crush at Dover, there'd be no reason for anyone to notice him particularly.'

'What about currency, though? Suppose he could have applied for it in the normal way, but there'd be a record of that, wouldn't there? Entered in his passport or something, eh?'

'It's quite likely he had a little over from some earlier trip. If he took some food with

252

him, he could have managed with very little.'

'And then?' Henry said. 'I mean when he got there.'

'Well, it's a goodish walk from the station to the villa, but not too far,' Alistair said. 'Rose and I walked down from the villa to the station without giving it a thought.'

'And he knew,' Henry said, 'that Pantelaras would have the coins in the villa that day. Oh dear. Suppose it's all possible so far. But what then? He gets in—yes, dare say that's possible. Pantelaras was very cagey about letting anyone in when he'd got his collection around, but he'd remember Paul from the time he lived here. So Paul gets in—then what?'

'He bashes Pantelaras's head in with a brass door-stop and walks out again with the collection and the gun that he's found in the house.'

'But look here—look here—that won't do!'

'Why not?'

'Because . . .' Henry disentangled himself from Agnes, absently thrusting her towards a chair. 'Because—well, customs. What about the customs?'

'Just one more risk that he decided to take,' Alistair said, 'though perhaps the biggest of them. All the same, how often, when you've been travelling, have you had your

253

pockets searched by the customs?'

'My pockets? Can't say I remember it ever happening to me. No, I don't think so.'

'It's never happened to me or to Rose,' Alistair said.

'But a collection of coins, you know—that isn't just a handful of change.'

'Couldn't it have been stowed in the pockets of a mackintosh and a suit—perhaps in the linings too?'

'Perhaps, perhaps. Yes, I suppose that's possible. But the gun—why did he take the gun?'

'That must have been unpremeditated. He may have thought that if he did lose the gamble and was searched, he'd prefer to be able to put an end to things on the spot.'

'Yes, shouldn't wonder. Yes, I can understand that. But he gets away with it, comes home, settles down again as if nothing had happened— No, by God, he doesn't!' Henry slapped his thigh. 'No, he goes into his studio and makes that terra-cotta thing of Pantelaras. I'll never forget the shock that gave me. You know, he must have been mad. Yes, that's the only possible explanation. Must have been mad as they come. And here we were, living right next to him for years and never suspecting it. Because what could he want with the collection? Never had the least interest in that sort of thing, that I remember.'

'But he was interested in money.'

Henry frowned. The word might have been one with which he was not really familiar.

'You think so? Always thought he had plenty, but I suppose nobody has, really. Never enough, eh? Perhaps, perhaps. But then what? He gets murdered himself. Someone works all this out, gets in and shoots him, makes off with the coins—that the idea?'

As Alistair nodded, Mrs. Bycraft returned from the kitchen with coffee and some toast and butter and marmalade on a tray. Her coffee was a curious brew, but it was hot. Drinking it made Alistair hungry and he started on the toast and marmalade, but Rose would not eat anything at all. Henry fussed around them until he saw that they both had all they wanted, then he returned, with quiet, heavy persistence, to his questioning.

'But who was that, eh? Who knew he had the coins? Who knew he had the gun? Or didn't he know about the gun? Didn't he mean to do a murder? And when did it happen? They're able to make pretty good guesses at that sort of thing, aren't they? Then they'll start asking us all where we were and so on. I wonder where Agnes and I were. Because she's quite right, you know, it could have been me. I mean, if I'd known Paul had the coins, I almost might have murdered him. Not only to get hold of them, but because of poor old Pantelaras. Some people didn't take to him, but I understood him. Had a lot of fellow-feeling. Poor old fellow. Well, when did it happen, Alistair?'

'My own guess,' Alistair said, 'is that it happened during the thunderstorm.'

'That so? Well, if you're right, I needn't worry. Nor need any of us here. All sweltering in that confounded tent, eh? But why d'you think it happened then?'

'Well, it happened then or later,' Alistair said. 'It happened after the rain started, because Paul's muddy footmarks are all over his kitchen floor. He must have been in the studio when the rain began, have gone to the house, gone in by the back door, walked to the sink, then gone from there to the sitting-room, and let his murderer in quite soon after that, because he never went back to the kitchen.'

'How d'you make that out?'

'Because all the footmarks are quite sharp and clear. If he'd walked across any of them, they'd have smudged.'

Henry looked inquiringly at Agnes, who

nodded, confirming that this was indeed what would have happened.

'But why d'you think it happened during the storm and not much later?' he asked. 'The ground stayed muddy for some time after that downpour.'

'Well, if it happened while it was thundering so loudly, that explains why none of us heard the shot.'

'Ah,' Henry said. 'See what you mean. Yes, of course. Well, I hope for all our sakes that's when it happened. It'll clear a lot of people. That tent must have held three-quarters of the village.'

'A tentful of alibis,' Agnes said. 'How fortunate. But suppose it happened later. Who has alibis then?'

'You and I,' Henry answered, 'were working at clearing up the field until about seven o'clock that evening. Lucky for us it was one of your good days.'

She gave one of her whooping laughs. 'See what a guilty conscience he's got? Justifying himself before anyone's accused him of anything. Ah, Henry, how you'd have loved those coins, wouldn't you? How you must wish you'd known all this, and thought of murdering Paul yourself!'

Alistair saw Henry shrink, as if the words had touched a nerve that was more sensitive than Henry would have been prepared to admit.

They had touched something in Rose as well. With a clumsy movement, she set down her cup, banging it against its saucer and spilling some coffee. Then she started rubbing with her handkerchief at the drops on her skirt, looking hard and frowningly at what she was doing.

Mrs. Bycraft merely said, 'Well!' She looked with angry dislike at Agnes. But this was the expression that had been on her face ever since she had returned from the kitchen, and Alistair thought it probable that she had overheard what Agnes had said of her work. With his own tolerance at a low ebb, he found it difficult not to tell Agnes to keep her mouth shut. The arrival of the police a few minutes later came actually as a relief.

Irene arrived with them, darting swiftly into the room ahead of the inspector and going straight to Rose. Irene, Alistair thought, had cried, but not a great deal, and she had already repaired her make-up. But her eyes looked very large and shadowy in her pale face.

Alistair was the first to be questioned by Lack, who had borrowed for the purpose the tiny room that was called Henry's study. From the start it was the murder in Monte

Carlo that Lack wanted to discuss, and it was he, not Alistair, who brought in the Griffins' name, asking for a repetition of what Alistair had told the police in Floxsted about the anonymous letter. When he had concluded this, Alistair added to it the story of the appearance of a silver decadrachm of Syracuse on the Joy Wheel at the Rollway village fête, and laid the coin on the desk before the superintendent.

He told Lack what Henry had told him of the coin and of the talk that Rose and he had had with the Griffins in the Red Lion in Floxsted. He told Lack all over again how he had discovered Paul Eckleston's body. He spoke of Paul's passport and said most of what he had just been saying to Henry and Agnes.

In spite of a peevish manner, Lack was very quick and had an amazingly retentive memory. At the end he asked Alistair if he had noticed the muddy footmarks in the kitchen. Also he asked him for an account of how he had spent his time the day before, from midday until six in the evening.

Questioned in his turn by Alistair, Lack said that the present state of the body suggested that the murder had happened during that span of time, and he agreed that the footmarks could probably be taken as limiting it further.

After Alistair, Rose was questioned, and after her, Mrs. Bycraft. It seemed to go on for hours. At about one o'clock, Agnes produced some sandwiches and more coffee, then complained about her back and went to lie down. It was early afternoon before Rose and Alistair, taking Irene with them, were able to go home.

When they started out, Irene was still unnaturally quiet. Alistair could not decide whether or not she was grieving. She seemed unaware of anything around her, but her delicate face looked hard as china, with only the eyes intensely, fiercely alive. It was Rose who looked sad, so sad that he felt it almost unbearable to look at her.

They walked home by a path across the park to a turnstile that led out on to the road a little outside the village. This meant a longer walk home, but avoided passing the lodge and the crowd that still stood curiously outside the gates.

Irene walked ahead and seemed to have no wish for comfort or for company. But when they reached the stile, she turned and looked at Alistair.

'Well then, who *did* do it?' she demanded, as if she supposed that he could tell her and had been deliberately tantalising her by

260

refusing to do so.

Rose answered her, 'The Griffins.'

'Are you demented?' Irene asked harshly.

'No,' Rose said with a snap in her voice. 'It has to be the Griffins.'

'That couple who walked in on your party? I don't believe they even knew Paul,' Irene said.

'I don't think they did,' Rose said, 'but they wanted something he'd got.'

'That *Paul* had got?' Irene's scornful tone said that if one thing was certain about Paul, it was that he possessed nothing whatever that could be worth even a minor quarrel, let alone murder. 'No, my dears, it might be nice for all of you here to be able to push it off on to a pair of strangers like that, but the police aren't going to swallow that.'

Rose glanced at Alistair. 'She doesn't know about the coins.'

'I know a lot about the coins,' Irene said. 'I've heard about nothing but those coins ever since I got here. But Paul had nothing to do with them.'

'Tell her,' Rose said to Alistair.

He did his best to do so as they stood grouped at the turnstile. Irene's intense glance rested on his mouth while he was speaking, and once or twice her own lips moved, as if she were murmuring his words

261

after him. When he finished she laughed abruptly.

'And that's Paul you've been talking about?' she said. 'You want me to believe that was Paul? Hell, didn't either of you *know* Paul?'

'I don't think you ever did,' Rose said.

'I knew him,' Irene said, 'even if I never could make up my mind what I felt about him.'

'Was that why you came?' Rose said. 'Was it to have another try at making up your mind?'

'What if it was?'

Alistair saw that unless something happened to stop it, the two of them would be quarrelling in another moment, quarrelling with all the savagery of their suffering nerves and a good deal of unadmitted jealousy.

He laid his hand on the turnstile. 'Let's go on.'

Irene swung herself through the turnstile, darted out into the road and stood looking back at them both, her arms rigid at her sides.

'I don't know what sort of fool you think I am,' she said. 'People always think I'm a fool, and I dare say they're right. But I lived with Paul for three years and I can tell you several things about him. He was selfish, he was self-

262

centred, he was stingy, but he wasn't cruel, he wasn't brutal and he didn't take risks. The only risk Paul ever took in his life was me—and how he regretted it! So you'd better think up something better to explain his murder than that he was a murderer himself.'

She spun on one heel and walked off down the road.

It was a moment before Rose followed her through the turnstile.

'It *was* the Griffins, wasn't it?' she said.

'More likely Griffin alone,' Alistair answered. 'Mrs. Griffin was at the fête all the afternoon, at least until we left it ourselves.'

'But she must have known about it.'

'One can't be sure.'

'I think one can. I think she was keeping an eye on us all while he searched our house, then went on to search Paul's.'

'And found Paul at home. All the same, I wonder how he knew Paul had the coins. He can't have known it beforehand, or he wouldn't have bothered to search our house at all. So something must have happened when he got to the lodge to give it away to him.'

'Don't you think the fact was simply that he recognised Paul?'

Alistair exclaimed, 'Why didn't I think of that before? Of course, if Paul was the mysterious stranger, seen by Robinet, he could easily have been seen somewhere in Monte Carlo by Griffin. And Griffin would purposely have left his description of him vague when he was talking to us, because by then Paul was dead already, and Griffin wouldn't have wanted to start us wondering about him. The longer he lay there, the harder it would be to say just when he was killed.'

'Yes, and that's why Paul left the fête as soon as he got there,' Rose said. 'He recognised Mr. Griffin. Since he didn't come to our party the evening before, they hadn't met there and Paul wouldn't have known anything about the Griffins' being here. But as soon as he arrived on the field, he saw them, and so left as fast as he could.'

Irene, still in front of them, stopped and faced them once more.

'The only thing about all that that's quite wrong,' she said, 'is that Paul didn't come to the fête at all.'

CHAPTER SIXTEEN

'He did,' Alistair said.

'He did not,' Irene answered. 'I was watching for him from the moment I got there, and I know he never came at all.'

'It was right at the beginning,' Alistair said, 'before you'd made your speech. You were standing by the cart, surrounded by people.'

'Did you see him yourself?'

'No, but Henry sold him a ticket.'

'That isn't true,' she said. 'He never came at all. Your Henry's lying.'

She swung away from them again and hurried on. When they reached the house she went straight upstairs and shut herself into her room.

Because she did this, she did not see what Rose and Alistair saw as they came in at the gate. The two Griffins were seated in the chairs under the cherry tree.

They stood up when they saw Rose and Alistair, but they did not come to meet them. Side by side, they waited in the shadow of the tree. Mrs. Griffin was dressed, with unusual sobriety, in grey, without any beads at all. Her soft pink face had the rigid look of a jelly

265

that has set a little too hard. Her husband seemed to be holding himself still by a great effort, but like a spring wound up too tight, looked ready at the first slip of control to whip out into wild movement.

Alistair was not at all glad to see them. The right people to talk to the Griffins, he thought, were the police.

'You might have waited in the house, since you know your way about it,' he remarked.

Mr. Griffin made a jerky gesture, dismissing that matter.

'You know why we're here, of course,' he said. 'We heard of the murder. We realise our positions may be awkward. We've found ourselves in the neighbourhood of a murder twice in remarkably swift succession. Coincidence, of course. And the police recognise that coincidences occur, but they're liable, naturally, to investigate them with a good deal of suspicion. So my wife and I would be very much obliged if you would tell us one thing.'

Alistair did not reply, but waited for the question.

'When did the murder happen?' Mr. Griffin demanded.

'The police have been asking us all what we were doing between midday and six o'clock yesterday,' Alistair said.

'That's unfortunate.'

'Yes.'

'I shan't find that question easy to answer.'

'No.' Alistair wished they would go. This man, he thought, was almost certainly a murderer, and it was a great strain, he discovered, to talk to a man who was almost certainly a murderer. Besides, he wanted to be alone with Rose.

Mr. Griffin went on, 'My wife, of course, can account for the whole of that time, but in my account there is necessarily the gap when I was being so foolish as to search your house.'

'So I realised.'

A gleam of cold humour came into Mr. Griffin's eyes. 'I can see you don't want to make the situation less difficult for us than it is. Well, my dear—' He turned to his wife. 'I think we had better go and have a talk with the police. We are not very welcome here, and though it will certainly be embarrassing, trying to explain to the police just why I was doing what I was between the time I left the field and the outbreak of the storm, still it seems to me more dignified to go looking for them than to have our unwilling host informing them of our whereabouts.'

Rose took a step forward. 'Did you say the *outbreak* of the storm?'

267

'Yes, just as the rain began, I was so fortunate as to catch a bus for Floxsted in the middle of the village. I'd left the car at the field, meaning to return there and wait for my wife, when I'd done in your house. But as I was walking towards the field the storm broke, and there was a bus stopping right beside me. So, to save a wetting, I jumped on board.'

'Was there anyone else in the bus?' Alistair said.

'Oh yes, a number of people.'

'Do you think any of them will remember you?'

'I can't say for certain, but when I got off the bus outside the Red Lion, that elusive female, who manages the hotel, was in the hall and confided in me that she was frightened of thunder and couldn't bear to stay alone in her office. May I ask the point of these questions?'

Alistair was unwilling to be convinced by the answers he had been given, because if he were to give up his suspicions of the Griffins there would be many things that he would have to attempt to think out all over again. And somewhere, possibly, something had been left out. At the same time, he saw that if the answers were truthful, he probably owed the Griffins an explanation.

268

'It seems likely,' he said, 'that Paul Eckleston was alive when the storm began. His muddy footprints are all over his kitchen floor.

Mrs. Griffin gave a crow of thankfulness.

'I knew it—I knew we oughtn't to worry,' she cried. 'It's wrong to worry when you've nothing on your conscience.'

'I have a little matter of breaking and entering, or whatever it's called, on my conscience,' her husband said. 'But more than ever now, I think we should go in search of the police.'

'Mr. Griffin,' Rose said abruptly, 'did Mr. Eckleston have lunch with you yesterday?'

Alistair could make no sense of this question. He had no idea of what she had in her mind when she asked it, and in so far as it delayed the departure of the Griffins out of the garden and out of their lives, he regretted it.

'Certainly not,' Mr. Griffin said. 'My wife and I had lunch together in the hotel—the sort of lunch which one would be happy to forget, but which nevertheless remains painfully fixed in the memory.'

'Did you have any appointment with Mr. Eckleston yesterday morning?' Rose asked insistently.

'My dear young lady, until I heard this

269

morning of his murder, I didn't even know of the existence of Mr. Eckleston.' Mr. Griffin slipped his arm through his wife's. She looked as if at that point she had suddenly thought of a number of things that she would like to say, but he hustled her away.

So at last the thing had happened for which Alistair had been craving all day. He and Rose at last were alone. Indeed, they were very much alone. As he dropped into one of the chairs under the cherry tree, where Paul had so often sat with them that summer, it came to him that perhaps they were alone in a way that they had never been before, and that he did not know at all what this being alone was going to mean.

Putting off the moment of discovery, thrusting a hand through his hair, he asked Rose why she had asked the Griffins if Paul had had lunch with them.

She sat down in a chair facing him, and gazed upwards into the green, still shade.

'Didn't you notice?' she said. 'There were no used dishes in the kitchen, and I think that means that Paul went out for lunch. He was quite good at looking after himself generally, but he was an untidy person, he didn't wash up or put things away. So if he'd had lunch at home, there would have been some plates and things in the sink.'

Alistair still could not see that it was important. But as he sat there in the quiet of the afternoon, with a bee bumbling past and the air full of sweet, drowsy scents, importance seemed to drain out of almost everything, leaving only one or two things starkly present in his thoughts, things which could not be dodged any longer.

'Rose, let's go back to the real reason why you believed Paul murdered Pantelaras,' he said. 'You know, if I hadn't seen his passport, I don't think I'd believe it even now. But you believed it without having seen the passport.'

She brought her gaze down to his face. 'I told you, it was in that letter he wrote to me when we were at Cap Martin.'

'I simply can't believe that.'

'Why not?'

'Well, did you ever say anything about it to him when we got back?'

'Of course.'

'And what did he say?'

'He denied that he'd ever written to me.'

'And that's really why you began to think that he must have been the murderer of Pantelaras—because he lied about that.'

'I suppose so, yes. He got so angry. He seemed to think I was setting some sort of trap for him. He challenged me to produce the letter—knowing, of course, that I shouldn't be able to.'

'How could he know that?'

'It wasn't the sort of letter one would keep.' She gave a shuddering sigh. 'It was a horrible letter.'

'And this happened—this talk you had—the day I was away in London, the day the Griffins sent us the picture of the owl?'

'Yes, he went away in a rage with me, pretending he thought I was trying to induce him to be treacherous to you. And that's the last time I saw him.'

He nodded, recognising that his guess that Rose and Paul had had some sort of showdown on that day, and that that had been the reason of her extreme tension in the evening, had been perfectly correct. Yet something about the recklessness of it all, of a letter to advertise his guilt, of his slapdash handling of Mrs. Bycraft, of his travelling so openly to perform his murder, seemed unlike Paul. They would have been the actions of a very stupid or very desperate man, and Alistair felt that he had no reason to regard Paul as either.

'I suppose there's no possibility that he was speaking the truth and that he didn't write that letter?' he said.

Rose's cheeks reddened.

'You saw it,' she said. 'You saw me reading it.'

'Yes,' he said.

'And you saw his passport to-day.'

'Yes.'

'Then what are you trying to say?'

'I don't know.'

He got up and began to walk up and down on the worn grass under the trees.

'I don't know, except that there's something about it all that doesn't add up,' he said. 'I know I've been busy all day proving very nicely that Paul murdered Pantelaras for the coins, and then that someone else—not Griffin, because of his alibi—came alone and murdered Paul for the same reason. But I'm haunted by a feeling that I've gone thoroughly wrong somewhere, that I've mixed up the important and the unimportant things, or somehow got everything upside down.'

Rose watched him calmly as he walked backwards and forwards.

'If it's Mr. Griffin's alibi that's worrying you,' she said, 'anyone can wear a pair of shoes.'

He reached up and tore a spray of leaves off the tree and gesticulated with it as he walked.

'You mean Griffin went there and shot Paul, then put on his shoes and deliberately made those footmarks before the rain had ever come?' he said. 'That would be a very subtle sort of alibi. But suppose that after it the rain hadn't come at all.'

'He could have been pretty certain that it would, watching that black cloud come up.'

'Not absolutely certain. The rain could have come down a few miles off, as it did last week.'

'He could have thought it worth trying.'

'Yes, but all the same . . . Rose, tell me more about that letter.'

He thought from the change in her face that she was going to flare up in anger, then he saw her lips curve into an uncertain smile.

'All right, I'll try to tell you what you really want to know,' she said. 'About Paul. About me. But sit down. For God's sake sit down!'

Taking hold of one of the chairs, for no particular reason he wrenched it to a different position, then sat down and slashed with the spray of leaves at a hovering mosquito.

'But it isn't going to be the easiest thing in the world to talk about,' Rose said, 'because really there's so *little* to talk about.'

'I know that.'

'No, not as I mean it. Oh, I know you know Paul and I weren't lovers. But you haven't been able to make up your mind how much we cared for each other, how much he mattered to me, how much he'd managed to alter my feelings about you, how much I was having to struggle with my own heart to stay loyal to you. And you couldn't bear to show even that amount of doubt.'

'*Even* that amount,' Alistair muttered.

'Ah, I know. But it was only when that letter came and you wouldn't read it that I became sure how much it all meant to you, and by then I was so confused myself. . . . I'd realised, that evening when you brought Henry home with you, that there was something wrong, but not how much you were hating it. Yet even before the letter came, I'd decided it had to stop. And when I got that letter . . .'

She sat up abruptly, pressing her hands to her temples.

'Listen,' she said, 'this may sound mad to you, knowing what you do now, but my idea of Paul, until he wrote that letter, was that he was a sensitive, lonely man, desperately afraid of real intimacy with anyone. He'd been hurt, I thought, perhaps by Irene, perhaps before that, and the one thing he was determined about was that he'd never be hurt like that again. He wanted to have someone to whom he could talk a little about himself, and think of as caring about what he did and what happened to him, and he wanted to play, just a very little, at being in love with her. But at a breath of real response, the whole thing would have faded. I was quite sure that was how it was. And I was sorry for him and sometimes flattered, and sometimes simply angry because he was so afraid of me.'

'Of course,' Alistair said.

'Of course?' she echoed questioningly. 'You mean you think that *is* the truth about Paul?'

'I meant, of course you were angry.'

'Ah—particularly as I thought, you see, that really he liked you a good deal better than he did me. But there it turned out I was wrong, because that letter was an outburst of hate and jealousy against you. And he said that he knew I really loved him, and that if it weren't for your having more money than he had, I'd have left you and gone to him. It might have been pathetic if it hadn't been so ugly, because it was an obscene thing—extraordinarily obscene. And also it talked about Pantelaras and the coins.'

'Yet you answered it,' Alistair said.

'On a postcard.'

'Why answer it at all?'

'I told you this morning, mostly to annoy you, because you wouldn't help me sort things out. That was childish, wasn't it? But also I answered because I thought—it seemed the only thing to think—that Paul was insane. Quite tragically insane and that there wasn't any point in being angry.'

He had been watching Rose intently, but now, fanning himself with the spray of leaves in his hand, he watched the movements of a robin that was making some bold little sorties after crumbs close to their feet.

'What you haven't said,' he said after a moment, 'is that you were fond of Paul.'

'Well?' she said.

'It must have hurt to lose him—I mean, through that letter.'

'Yes.'

'But suppose—just suppose—he didn't write that letter.'

She flung up her hands in exasperation.

'You saw it, you saw it!'

'It was typewritten, wasn't it? And he had the showy sort of signature that's the easiest to forge.'

'But why should anyone do that?'

'I—I'm not sure. But I think . . .' He stood up restlessly and began to walk up and down again. 'I think that's what must have happened. I can't believe that Paul wrote that letter, and I feel more than ever that there's something all wrong about the way we've been adding two and two together. I think someone else wrote the letter, knowing just

277

how you'd react to it. Someone who knows you pretty well.'

'But *why*?'

'To make you think just the things that you've been thinking. To help prepare a case against Paul for the murder of Pantelaras, which you'd be convinced by in advance.'

'But suppose I'd kept the letter, and we could show that it was a forgery.'

'You said yourself it was the sort of letter one wouldn't keep.'

'I'm afraid I still don't understand,' she said. 'I think you're trying very hard to make things easier for me—but there's still the proof in his passport, isn't there? There's still the fact that he went to France.'

'Unless,' Alistair said, 'the truth is that Paul didn't go to France in fact, perhaps hardly left his studio all that week-end. Suppose it was someone else who travelled on his passport.'

Rose did not take it in at once. Her eyes widened, but without expression. Then he saw the flash of awareness in them.

'But there's only one person who could possibly—' she began excitedly. 'Unless you mean—no, you can't mean, can you, that it was a joint passport, for husband and wife? Surely it couldn't be, after all this time.'

'No, it wasn't a joint passport,' he said.

278

'I've been thinking about Irene, wondering if she fitted in anywhere, but I'm sure she doesn't, and for some of the same reasons I can't convince myself Paul really fits in. You see, we've been talking about his wanting money badly, but even if he did, was ten thousand pounds really enough to tempt him to take the enormous risk of that murder and robbery? Because those risks were really so immense that only an absolutely desperate man would have taken them. Isn't that so? Think of the journey home! God, I wouldn't have faced that journey for all the money in the world. And the collection wouldn't have realised ten thousand pounds if it was sold under cover, but probably only a quite small fraction of it.'

'A desperate man,' Rose said. 'Yes—yes, I see. But not for money.'

'No, not for money.'

'And if you're right, Paul didn't . . .'

'Didn't murder anyone, or write that letter.'

He saw her eyes fill with tears. As they spilled over and slid down her cheeks, Alistair bent and kissed her. She caught at his hand and held on to it tightly.

'But I still don't understand—' she began.

'I think I'd better have a quiet talk with Mrs. Bycraft,' he said. 'Want to come?'

'No, I think I'd better go to Irene,' she said.

He nodded and walked quickly away.

CHAPTER SEVENTEEN

The entrance to Purslem Manor, approached from the great avenue, was through a wide archway that led into a paved courtyard. Facing the archway across the courtyard was another lower and narrower archway, leading into an inner court. The buildings around this were the oldest part of the house. Alistair had once been taken all over them by Henry, but it was only the great hall that was open to the public, a tremendous room with age-blackened beams and ancient trestle tables, long enough to seat a hundred retainers, along each side of the room. Suits of armour, labelled with the names and dates of their probable owners, stood in the corners. There was no fireplace. A few inconspicuous radiators slightly reduced the chill of the room in winter and helped to keep it dry, but a pile of logs, arranged in the middle of the worn stone floor, showed how the hall would once have been heated. Only a little less of an anachronism than the radiators, the wonderful Van Dyke of a Purslem who had fought for the king, hung high on the end wall.

On any normal summer Sunday afternoon, when cars and charabancs were parked three deep at the main entrance, there would have been twenty or thirty people wandering about the great hall, waiting there for guides to take them farther. They would have filled in the time exclaiming at the heating arrangements, comparing their own heights with those of the suits of armour, and gazing up, stirred beyond their own understanding, at the long handsome face, the glowing velvet and fine lace in the famous portrait.

To-day the hall was empty. There were no charabancs at the entrance. The iron-studded gates inside the first archway were closed, and if the porter there had not known Alistair and that his claim that he had important business with Mr. Wallbank was likely to be true, even the wicket gate would not have been unbolted for him.

Henry's office was about ten minutes' walk away from the hall, or so it had always seemed to Alistair, whenever he had made his way along the dark passages and up the steep narrow stairs, then through the panelled galleries, with the furniture of five centuries ranged along them, with only some looped red cords to protect it from the desire, often felt by the general public, to test the comfort of some chair, covered in ragged and faded but still lovely Jacobean upholstery. On the walls here hung row on row of pictures, among which there was a probable Holbein, two Gainsboroughs and also a large number of the signed works of the late Miss Caroline Purslem, 1833–1904, who had liked to paint thatched cottages with herbaceous borders. For that was the nature and also the fascination of the Purslem Collection. Miss Caroline, her aunts and great-aunts and others long before them, had all made their contributions to the treasure, as far back as, and even beyond, the woman whose name was unknown, but whose cookery book, in the difficult writing and dim ink of the sixteenth century, was in a glass case in the ballroom, always open at a recipe for cooking peacocks in honey.

At last, beyond the galleries, beyond the state bedrooms and down and up another staircase, that led to a more modern wing, and through a door marked Private, the person who really knew his way about would discover Henry's office. He had chosen a small room for himself. At least, it always appeared small to anyone who had come through the halls and galleries. Its walls were covered in blue Italian damask, its two tall windows overlooked the pleasantest sweep of the park, and the delicate carving of the ceiling was not by Grinling Gibbons. The fact that it appeared to be necessary to state that the carving was *not* by Grinling Gibbons, because it was so good that it almost migh[t] have been, had made a great impression o[n] Alistair. He envied Henry that office. Bu[t] without question it was the only thing that he had ever envied Henry.

He did not actually say so to Henry to-day, yet he spoke with a certain sympathy which came from the sense that every man has a right to be envied for more than his office ceiling. Yet if it is not possible to do so, if a man, in fifty-five years of life, has garnered nothing for himself but, legally and worthily, an office with a beautiful ceiling, and by murder and robbery, a small but choice collection of Greek coins, one must not, Alistair thought, allow one's sympathies to carry one away. There is more the matter than bad luck, even the incredible bad luck of being married to Agnes, a photograph of whom, young and quite pretty, with shingled hair and shy, intelligent eyes, was on the table, always at Henry's elbow.

But Henry, so far, was making no demands for sympathy. He had nodded his bald head at intervals while Alistair had talked. He had argued very little. He had even shown, it seemed to Alistair, a sort of satisfaction in hearing the story of his own crime.

'Yes,' he said at last. 'Yes, see what you mean. You've talked to Mrs. Bycraft about hat week-end, realised she never saw me, although she was working for Agnes. Very shrewd of you. And you've realised about the passport. Yes. And the police have only got to start thinking along those lines and I'm done for. Finished. Naturally. That chap in Monte Carlo, the one they've got in gaol, he'll identify me. There'll be people on the boat, on the train. They can always find them, can't they, once they know what they're looking for? And I suppose they'll pull the place apart too, looking for the coins. Well, they needn't look far. Somehow felt I mightn't have them long, so thought I'd have them where I could see them whenever I felt like it. Look!'

He pulled open the drawer of the table before him, thrust both hands in and brought them out filled with silver coins.

Dropping them on the blotter in front of him, he bent his head above them, then ran a hand over them tenderly, as if he were softly stroking the hair of someone he loved.

'Haven't had time to arrange them yet,' he said. 'I just slip a hand in sometimes and touch them. Like to feel them, you know. Here, look at this one. Look at the face, the wreath. . . .'

He had picked one up from the heap and was holding it out to Alistair. His eyes behind the crooked spectacles were sparkling.

Alistair drew back sharply.

Henry sighed. 'Ah. Don't suppose you understand, really. And there's a lot to clear up, of course. One or two points I'd like cleared up myself, as a matter of fact. Those muddy footmarks, now. Could have knocked me over with a feather when you showed how Paul couldn't have been killed till after the rain started, when I knew damn' well it was around half past twelve when I killed him. Remember how they were testing out the loudspeaker on the field around then, making all sorts of queer cracks and bangs? That's why no one took any notice of the noise of the shot. It wasn't the thunderstorm. But I didn't argue the point naturally, since it gave Agnes and me a perfect alibi—far better than my pretending I'd seen Paul on the field in the afternoon. Pity I ever said that, eh? Must have been one of the things that tipped you off about me, when you realised when he really was killed. But explain about those footmarks, Alistair. How did they get made when Paul was dead?'

'There are two ways of making muddy footmarks,' Alistair answered. 'One is with muddy feet. But the other is with dry, dusty feet on a wet floor. And the last thing that Mrs. Bycraft did that morning, before she went home, was scrub the kitchen floor, and she's a rather messy worker, if one believes Agnes, and sloshes a good deal of water around. Then, as soon as she'd gone, Paul came in from the studio to keep the appointment he'd made with you, went to the sink to wash his hands, then went into the sitting-room, and left that trail of footmarks on the clean floor.'

'Interesting,' Henry said. 'Really is. Only thing is, it only shows Paul may not have been alive when the storm began. Doesn't show conclusively that he wasn't.'

'No, but he never had any lunch, you know,' Alistair said. 'I checked with Mrs. Bycraft that if he'd had any, there'd have been some plates and things in the sink. He didn't wash up for himself. He was a believer in stacking.'

'Great mistake,' Henry said. 'Unhealthy. Never do it at home. So you realised he was killed before he'd had any lunch, and so my statement that he'd come on to the field in the afternoon had to be a lie, eh? Yes, I see.' He was still gazing at the coin that he had picked up, holding it close to his eyes with the sharpened look of concentration that came into them when they dwelt on an ancient and precious thing. 'I'll tell you something, Alistair. Never believed in my heart I'd get away with any of it, even as long as I have. But all the same, I've had my beauties a week—no, nine days, a whole nine days. All to myself.'

His calm voice shook. He put the coin down on the blotter and with gentle fingers picked up another.

'Remarkable how it all worked out, though, from the time Pantelaras first wrote, out of the blue, offering his collection as a gift to the Purslem. Didn't even know before he wrote where he was living. Trouble was, as soon as I began to think it over, I found I wanted the thing for myself. Wanted it badly. Wanted it so badly I couldn't sleep at nights. Just for a change, you see, I wanted something rare and beautiful and valuable that I could call my own, the sort of thing I might have had, too, if I'd been a naturally ruthless man like Pantelaras.'

'There's something rather ruthless about murder,' Alistair suggested.

'That's what Agnes said. Almost her words! "Why not be a bit ruthless yourself for once?" she said. She said she'd respect me more if I was a bit ruthless occasionally. Odd, that. She understood it was on her account I'd gone without some things I'd very much have liked to have. Well, naturally I had. You do, for a person you love. Still, she wanted me to go out and get myself something for a

288

change—whatever the consequences. Very odd really, how much she wanted it, almost as if she despised me for not having done it before.'

'So Agnes put you up to it.'

Henry started slightly and frowned. 'I didn't say that. We worked it out together. I'm not very clever myself. Not very practical. For instance, the first problem was how to get Pantelaras to bring his coins out of the bank without appearing on the scene myself. Well, Agnes solved that. "The Dirkes are going to Cap Martin," she said, "get them to go and see him." So then we thought up a reason why I might ask you to go and see him, and that's why I told you he'd offered to sell the coins, when the fact was, of course, he meant them to be a gift, to spite his daughter. But their being a gift wouldn't do, because with my knowing the collection as I did, all I'd got to do was accept it. No reason to send an ambassador, no sense in it. So we made up the yarn about his having offered the collection for a queer sort of sum that wasn't anything like its real value, but big enough that one wouldn't spend it without investigating things pretty carefully first. Cunning, eh? And we told Pantelaras you were a collector and a friend of mine and mighty interested in his coins, and I arranged for you to see him late on the Friday.'

'Having been very insistent, I remember,' Alistair said, 'that you'd make all the arrangements to save me trouble, when, in fact, it would really have been far easier to make them myself.'

Henry smiled. 'Yes, that worked very nicely. And I arrived on the Friday in the morning. Travelled by train—less conspicuous than plane, of course—and used Paul's passport. Matter of fact, that was where the whole idea began, you know that I could easily travel on Paul's passport. He always left everything lying about, no difficulty in getting hold of it, and with a little make-up—eyebrows, I mean, and his sort of spectacles—it was simple. I've got his bald head, you see. Older than him, of course, but he looked much older than he was, and it was a bad photograph, as they always are. Well, I got to Monte Carlo, pretty tired, but had a good breakfast, then waited around till I was pretty sure Pantelaras would have been to the bank, then I walked up to his villa. He recognised, me, in fact, he was delighted to see me.'

'And you hit him over the head with a brass doorstop,' Alistair said. 'He was old and very frail. He couldn't have put up a fight.'

290

Henry's features twitched. 'He was a ruthless man. No heart, no love for anyone. He never denied himself anything he wanted for the sake of anyone else.'

'He was what you'd like to be yourself,' Alistair said.

'You're wrong, quite wrong!' Henry cried out, suddenly excited. 'I'm not like that at all. Not in the least.'

'Well, go on,' Alistair said. 'You planted the letter from yourself that gave the same version of what I was going to see him about as you'd given me, then you cleared out with the coins and the gun.'

'Yes—and the gun,' Henry said. 'You were quite right about that this morning, though you thought it was Paul who'd taken it. It came on me suddenly, while I was in that house, just what risks I was running. You know, until I'd actually killed Pantelaras, I didn't really believe I seriously meant to do it. It felt as if I were playing some sort of game. And I could have called it off at any minute. But when I'd done it and was just going to leave the house, I suddenly thought of what would happen if they went through my luggage carefully at the customs. So when I saw the gun, I took it, to end it quickly, you know, if I was caught on the journey. But I lost my head rather at that point, and forgot to lock the door or the gate when I left. Didn't make that mistake when I shot Paul. Went round and locked up everything carefully.'

'Except the studio.'

Henry looked vexed. 'Dear me, did I forget that?'

'And all the time that you were abroad,' Alistair said, 'you were supposed to be ill in bed.'

'That's right. Some of Agnes's planning, that. I've no head for detail. I'd just have taken the passport and gone, and trusted to luck Paul would never notice the date-stamps, or if he did, that he'd think they were just some blundering official's mistake, and had been made long before. I'd asked him, that evening in your garden, if he was going abroad this summer and he'd said no, so I didn't think he'd notice the passport was missing for a few days. But when I said that to Agnes, she said it wasn't good enough. She said if Paul got suspicious, we might find we'd got to get rid of him, and that the clever thing would be to have a case all ready, so that he'd then get blamed for the murder of Pantelaras. So the first thing she did was borrow Mrs. Bycraft from him for the Saturday. She'd spread it around already I was ill, so that people wouldn't think anything at my being away from the Purslem for a few days, and having Mrs. Bycraft to help her supported that story, at the same time as seeing that Mrs. Bycraft didn't see Paul between the Wednesday and the Monday.'

'And Agnes kept Mrs. Bycraft busy downstairs, doing the floors and the downstairs windows,' Alistair said. 'She wouldn't let her tidy your room or carry up a tray.'

'No, of course not. That wouldn't have done at all. But d'you know what else Agnes did?'

'She wrote Rose a letter.'

'Oh, yes, that. No, I meant about the milk,' Henry said. 'Subtle touch. She put a notice on Paul's doorstep late at night, telling the milkman not to leave any milk for three days. Then she asked him for extra milk for ourselves and as soon as it was delivered, she nipped down and put it on Paul's doorstep. Ask the milkman, he'll tell you Paul was away for three days, but Paul himself never knew anything about it. Of course, someone else might have seen Paul during the weekend. Couldn't guard against that. But you know how he used to vanish into his studio for days at a time, and I'd dropped a hint about having an exhibition of his work up here, and I knew that'd make him go at it extra hard.'

'Henry, that letter,' Alistair said slowly and carefully. 'It was a mistake.'

Henry frowned, impatient at the interruption. He had been telling his story eagerly, with triumph in his voice. He wanted the exaltation of the moment to last, to conceal for as long as possible the coming moment of collapse.

'It helped to make you suspicious of Paul, didn't it?' he said.

'Yes, but clever as it was, and intimately as Agnes must have understood the relationship between the three of us to be able to write it, that letter led to a serious quarrel between Rose and Paul. Rose said some things that hurt Paul's feelings very badly, as a result of which he decided to go abroad. And so he started looking for his passport and couldn't find it. Then he caught you in his house and you said you'd come to tell him about the rumour about Tolliver's onions, and also you put on an act, to distract his attention, of being shocked at that figure of Pantelaras. Or perhaps, I don't know, you really were shocked. Then you left and he put the figure away in a bureau, and while he was doing it—this is what I'm sure happened—he saw the passport you'd just returned. I remember he started to talk very oddly then, as if his mind wasn't on what he was saying, and after

I'd gone he rang you up and made an appointment to see you next day. And you went along, taking the gun with you. Whose idea was that, Henry, yours or Agnes's?'

Henry's high forehead wrinkled. The brightness went out of his gaze. As vague and bewildered as usual, it dwelt on the pile of coins on the blotter, as if he wondered what on earth they were doing there.

'Really I don't know,' he muttered. 'Doesn't make much difference now, does it? Meant it to be taken for a suicide, of course, but blundered somehow. Smashing that figure of Pantelaras—was that a mistake? Couldn't stand it staring at me, had to smash it to bits. Told you, I'm no good at details. Then I thought that man Griffin had turned up providentially. Thought for sure he'd get suspected. Well, well. Agnes and I were both in it together, of course. Very close to each other always. Always did everything together. Only she would laugh at the wrong moment, couldn't cure her of it. Too highly strung.'

'That was just cracking the whip at you, Henry, reminding you of her power over you,' Alistair said. 'I think she must have enjoyed organising murder. She thrived on it. I'm not so sure about you. You've not looked too good lately. I noticed it particularly when we arrived at the show. Now I know why, of course.'

'Wonderful woman,' Henry said dreamily. 'She always said, if it went wrong, we'd end it together. Hope that'll be possible. Alistair . . .'

Alistair stood up quickly. He did not want to have to reply to what he thought was coming next. He did not want even to hear it.

'I'm just going, Henry,' he said.

'To the police?'

'Yes.'

'Yes. Yes, of course. Very considerate of you to have come here first.'

Alistair started for the door. He knew that he had not been considerate. For once he too, thinking of Rose and of himself, had been ruthless, as ruthless as Pantelaras, perhaps even as ruthless as Henry. And he felt cold and sick, but he did not regret it. Rose and he had their desperate needs just then, as desperate as ever Henry's had been for that heap of old metal on the blotter.

'There's just one thing that occurs to me,' Henry was continuing. 'That decadrachm you showed me. It's my opinion that that's properly the property now of the Rollway Village Produce Association. That Griffin woman gave it to the Boley child, and he wagered and lost it on the Joy Wheel. No great value, of course, in its present condition, but that being so, why shouldn't it be used, suitably mounted, as a prize at next year's show? Not this year's. Wouldn't want it to go to that rascal Tolliver for his spring-sown onions. But it's a head of Persephone, you know. The fertility of the earth. Very appropriate really, and quite remarkably beautiful. . . .'

He was still mumbling as Alistair let himself out of the room and went away quickly, down and up the stairs, through the state bedrooms, the halls and ballrooms and along the silent, splendid galleries.